We're all a little TIRED

you are enough

BOOK 2½

A NOVELLA BY
TIFFANY ANDREA

Paperback ISBN: 978-1-990724-12-1
Hardcover ISBN: 978-1-990724-13-8
eBook ISBN: 978-1-990724-14-5

Cover Design by: Burden of Proofreading Publishing featuring Graphics by Krisdog via CanStockPhoto

Interior Graphics by Yupriamos

This book is for the NICU staff at SickKids hospital who not only saved the life of our baby girl, Amaya, but did their best to comfort us in the process. You are real-life superheroes, and your care and compassion will never be forgotten.

Table of Contents

Preface

I want to preface this story by adding a trigger warning. If you're the type of person who isn't bothered by much in fictional writing, feel free to skip through and get started on the emotional roller coaster ahead. If you feel some potentially upsetting events could trigger you, please read the warning to ensure you're able to continue reading.

This story is one of trials related to pregnancy and childbirth. There is mention of a miscarriage, as well as babies in the neonatal intensive care unit (NICU). I tried to tackle both subjects in a way that allows people who have been through the same events could relate to. I would love this book to become a vehicle to drive the conversation forward regarding these difficult subjects. Too often we remain silent. We feel shame and heartbreak. We don't need to feel that alone.

I hope if you've felt the heartbreak addressed in this book, you find comfort in these pages. I hope you feel loved.

If you know someone who has been through similar struggles, I hope you show them love.

Love is the goal.

Trigger warning.

Head Over Heels

I

It's my big day.

Two years ago, I watched Liam walk across this stage, accepting his hard-earned diploma, ready to take on his future. My journey has been less straightforward, but here I am, preparing myself to take the same steps. I've gone in more of a zig-zag pattern, adding in a few spirals to keep things spicy, but despite being one of the older students in my graduating class, at the ripe old age of twenty-three, I'm proud of myself for getting here.

For most of my life, I didn't know what the future would entail, nor *who* I would have in it. As I look toward the massive crowd gathered to watch my convocation, I see my adoptive parents, Zach and Zara, my not-so-little sister, Isla, and the love of my life, Liam. He's been my best friend since high school, and I've been lucky enough to call him my boyfriend since the day he graduated.

He's been working hard at his job, helping the company to expand internationally, opening businesses in Europe and the United States. That, of course, requires him to travel occasionally, but it's given him the opportunity to purchase his first home, and I'm so proud of him for all he's accomplished. I hope I can make everyone proud of me, too.

I steady myself to cross the stage to obtain my degree in Drug and Addictions Counselling. When I started college at eighteen, I had been taking the Child and Youth Worker program, intending to work with kids in the foster care system. I thought that was where my passion was—helping kids like me. While on-the-job training is beneficial in most careers, my experiences led me to a different area of expertise. I unintentionally took on the role of drug addict, and that led me here. I've been clean for two years and focused on my studies, as well as continued to deal with my previous trauma. Now, I'm ready to be the person in someone else's corner.

My brief stint in rehab was life altering, and as a result, I wish to help others from a place of understanding and compassion. The next step to make that happen is interacting with the pot-bellied, middle-aged gentleman offering handshakes and fake diplomas in the centre of this stage.

When I hear my name, Chelsea Haynes, through the loudspeaker, I saunter forward. I shake the man's hand with my right, accept the paper with my left, and turn out toward the crowd. The mass of people causes me to freeze, but I look for the familiar faces of those I love. I find Zara smiling as she cheers from several rows back. Zach and Isla each flank her, beaming in my direction. The one person I wanted to make proud the most is missing.

My shoulders droop and I stalk forward to exit stage right. Walking, staring at the ground, I'm fighting back the tears threatening to escape. Liam wasn't even here to see my big moment.

"Chelsea."

I look up. Liam is on the stage. Why is Liam on the stage?

He drops to one knee in front of me, holding out a small velvet box.

I drop my diploma and run to tackle him without letting him get a word out. I don't think I could read this situation wrong. He's not up on the stage to tie his shoelace with a ring box.

Liam catches me as I assault him with a hug. I lean in to kiss his full lips, but he pulls away. "Hold on. I've been told I only have three minutes to do this, so you have to let me ask you the question."

I nod. Whoops.

"Chelsea." He clears his throat. "I thought the day I walked across this stage was the best day of my life. Not because of graduating, but because later that day, you told me you loved me for the first time. I was so wrong, though. Every day since has been better than the one before. So, I'm here, hoping to make your journey across this stage the best day of *your* life— so far. I hope I can make every day after today the best, over and over. Everything you've gone through to get here makes me proud to call you my girlfriend, but that's not enough. I want to call you my wife. If you'll have me, I want to love you forever."

Those tears that were threatening to pour out have been leaking down my face since Liam started speaking, and I'm ugly crying in front of a thousand captivated strangers. I don't care. I only saw him from a distance this morning since we arrived separately, but looking at him now, with his perfectly styled curly hair, his dewy caramel skin, and welcoming hazel eyes, he looks like home.

"Will you be my wife, Chels?"

I dive forward to tackle him again, right as he stands to envelop me in his arms. I don't worry about falling with him because I fell long ago, and he's always there to catch me.

"Yes. I choose you, Liam Davis. It was always you."

3

He slides a stunning oval cut solitaire diamond ring onto my left hand, and it's almost as beautiful as the man before me.

We exit the stage, hand in hand, to the cheers of onlookers who have no personal investment in our lives, but who doesn't *love* love? Well, I know a few people, but I will not waste my energy thinking about them.

Right now, I'm focusing on the man beside me who taught me how to love—who taught me how to trust.

Gut feeling

2

When Liam and I were married sixteen months ago, we had everything figured out. We created a to-do list with a carefully curated timeline in place so we could make the most of our life together, ticking off boxes most young married couples dream of. We purchased a home—which was infinitely easier with financially stable parents who insisted on pitching in as a wedding gift, and the equity from the home Liam purchased as a bachelor. We've done some travelling—something I never thought I'd do, but after a honeymoon road trip to New York City, it became something we enjoyed doing together—as long as we can drive. We both have jobs we love. Our relationship is stronger than ever.

The next logical step for us is to expand our family. As I stare down at the two pink lines on this life-changing bathroom chemistry experiment, I try to wrap my head around what this means for us.

Babies always change things. Dynamics between couples alter completely with a child in the picture. Which one of us will be the disciplinarian, and who will be the fun parent? Which one will the child gravitate toward or cry for when they skin their knee?

Is Liam going to be happy? This isn't in line with our timeframe, but we decided last month that we'd just not *not* try and see what happened. Turns out, we're fertile.

After walking into our open-concept kitchen, I seat myself in a plush, off-white barstool facing my laptop and take to the internet to find fun ways to spring the news on a spouse. I want this moment to be memorable—the moment our family no longer includes just us.

"We're going to give you a good life, baby," I mutter to my stomach.

Liam enters the kitchen after finishing his workout in our home gym—rather, *his* home gym. I don't go in there. I slam the laptop shut, not wanting him to see my internet search.

"What are you doing?"

"Oh. Um. Just googling something."

He quirks his brow, walking toward me. "Please don't tell me you're looking up some random symptoms for something. You know what my mom says about Dr. Google."

My mother-in-law is a family medicine practitioner at a clinic in Bracebridge. She's given me a few reminders over the years not to consult Dr. Google if something feels wrong.

"Well, not exactly." My face betrays my emotions before I've come up with a plan.

"What's wrong? I can call my mom."

"You're probably going to want to call her, but it's not what you think."

A frown emerges on Liam's face as he tilts his head. "Do you care to enlighten me? I'm stumped."

Before my mind can catch up with my mouth, I blurt, "we're pregnant."

He takes a second to absorb what I said. I berate myself for spoiling what was supposed to be a special moment. His eyes shoot wide open as he dashes toward me, scooping me off my stool in a bridal carry. "Are you serious? Pregnant? But, how?"

I giggle at his reaction. "Well, you see. When two people love each other…"

He kisses me to interrupt my absurdity. "I really do love you." He sets me on the white marble counter and crouches down in front of me, his face in line with my midsection. "I love your mom so much, little one. And I love you more than you'll ever know."

I stay perched in my position, taking in the scene before me, falling more in love with him by the second—and more in love with our baby.

I wipe a tear from his cheek, building the courage to ask something I know he won't be too fond of. "Can we keep this our little secret for a while? I don't know how far along I am, but I just want to get through the danger zone before we tell everyone."

Liam stands to face me. "Danger zone? Babe, I want to shout it from the rooftop." He backs up a few feet, throwing his hands in the air as he shouts, "I'm going to be a dad! Wooo!"

"You're such a goof." I chuckle, but quickly implement my serious face. "Let's just have our first appointment, and then we can tell everyone, okay?"

"I can't even tell my mom? She'll know everything we have to do and be able to point us in the right direction."

"Please, Liam. Not even your mom. Not yet."

"If that's what my baby-momma wants, then that's what she gets." His playfulness makes way for concern as he questions me. "Are you feeling okay? Do you feel any kicks yet? How come you don't look pregnant?"

"Wow, man. Slow down. First, I feel fine. No, I don't feel kicks or look pregnant because it's way too early. You're an impressive man, Liam Davis, but you didn't impregnate me with a fully formed fetus."

"I'm going to have to watch some YouTube videos about this or something. Oh, gosh. I don't know what I'm doing. What if I'm a terrible dad?"

I pause for a moment, thinking about the horrific things my father put me through as a child, and I can't imagine Liam being anything short of wonderful. I didn't have a mother figure in my life until Zara and Zach adopted me when I was fifteen. If either of us is going to fail as a parent, I'm confident it will be me. Despite my own fears of failure, I want to reassure Liam. "You're going to be a great dad. You'll be better than mine."

Liam cringes at the mention of my father. The demon-spawn, Kevin, is currently serving a twenty-five-year sentence for attempted kidnapping, drug possession, and a slew of other charges. Surely, anything is an improvement on that pedigree. That's not mentioning the things he did they didn't charge him with. His role as a failed parent has left me with a lifelong battle with PTSD and I have difficulty trusting people. I trust Liam.

"You had a good example for a father. You're a good man, and you're going to be an amazing dad. I know it."

"You're going to be a great mom, Chels. I can't wait to hold our baby in my arms. Hopefully it looks exactly like you."

I hope not. I look exactly like my father. The thought of recreating another human who reminds me of that monster terrifies me. Will I love our baby less if it resembles Kevin? Will red hair and freckles make me resent an innocent child just because of my past? I don't want to think it will, but it could happen. What if I hate my baby?

"What are you worried about?" Liam stops me from my pessimistic thought pattern.

WE'RE ALL A LITTLE TIRED

"Everything." Not a concise answer, but it's honest. I don't think I'm ready for this—the responsibility of raising another human, teaching them to be a good person, nourishing their mind and body. How can I ever be prepared for that?

"We'll face everything as a team. Whatever the future brings, we'll handle it together. Big Red and Arizona. Just like we always have." He leans in, placing a gentle kiss on my stomach, which I'm pretty sure is my intestines, but the sentiment is the same. "I love you, baby."

Heart Stopping

3

Keeping true to his word, Liam hasn't told anyone we are expecting, but I can tell he's eager to get through our appointment today so he can put up a billboard or something. He's beyond excited and it's endearing, but doesn't negate the fear I feel. Fear surrounding carrying and birthing a child, raising them, nurturing them. I'm not equipped with nurturing genes.

We're called into a small room where the technician directs me to the dressing room area, instructing me to change into a gown, but I'm allowed to keep my pants on—words I am happy to hear. Exposing my lower half never occurred to me. And, well, it's officially autumn.

When I walk back into our exam room, I find a waiting Liam and an overwhelmed technician. Liam has a habit of asking rapid-fire questions when he is nervous.

I lie back on the cold vinyl-covered table, the ridiculous tissue paper crinkling beneath me, and each movement is torture because of the volume of water I consumed before coming. This is some sort of cruel and unusual punishment. If they can send people into space, they should be able to take pictures of my uterus without my bladder threatening to burst.

With no warning, a cold jelly squirts onto my lower abdomen with an offensive sound, and the ultrasound tech is travelling a lot further south than I expected. I squirm under the pressure and because I'm so uncomfortable. I know he does this daily as his job, but he didn't even give me his name. Is this how it goes when you're pregnant? Suddenly your dignity goes out the window? As if squeezing a human out of your hoo-ha isn't bad enough.

The technician asks me for a third time to stay still and I mutter another apology. This is not the enjoyable, magical moment I imagined. All those movies lied.

Or maybe it *is* a magical moment and I'm not cut out for being a mom. I'm already being selfish; concerned about *my* bladder and *my* lady bits being on display, but I've forgotten why we're really here. I'm going to be terrible at this. My first mom-job and I've failed miserably.

After clearing his throat and adjusting the ultrasound probe again, the tech looks concerned.

"Is there a problem?" Liam asks.

"Do you know approximately how far along you are?" the man replies.

I already gave this information upon check-in, so I am certain he knows exactly what he's asking. He's avoiding the question.

"I think I'm about eleven weeks, give or take."

"Mm-hmm."

I shift again, but it's a response to the anxiety flooding my body. He hasn't shown us anything yet. He hasn't turned the screen our way or presented us with our perfect baby's heartbeat. The man issues me a look but, I'm assuming once he sees the glossiness of my eyes, he remains silent.

The look on the ultrasound technician's face confirms my fear long before he says any words. I think Liam knows too, because he's clenching my hand. A tear escapes my eye and runs into my ear. The sensation of the water droplet in my ear makes me shiver, and my excessively full bladder threatens to empty. This moment is already as horrible as I could imagine; I'd rather not pee myself, too.

"I'm going to get the doctor to discuss your results." The tall gentleman stands, sliding his wheeled stool back toward the wall and exits the room. His departure gives my tears the go-ahead they need.

From his position beside my head, Liam leans down to kiss my forehead. "Shh. Don't panic yet. Let's wait to hear from the doctor."

"No, I know. This isn't how it's supposed to go. He would have shown us something if there was good news. This is all my fault."

"Babe, nothing is your fault. If this wasn't meant to be, then we'll try again."

How can he even think about that? How can he just dismiss our child's life and act like it can be replaced so easily? Why didn't this baby ever get to experience how much we loved it. I cry even harder, realizing I referred to our first child as "it" and I'll never know otherwise.

The doctor eases her way into the room with a sombre expression. I gather she's given the same news to a lot of couples before, but it probably doesn't get easier to crush people's hearts.

"Mr. and Mrs. Davis."

Liam doesn't move nor let go of my hand. He's gazing at the doctor, but I've turned away to look at him. Navigating this scenario requires a familiar face.

12

"I'm sorry to tell you…"

I don't hear the rest of what she said. My sobs drown out all noises around me until a moment later, Liam lifts me up on the exam table and slides underneath my torso, pulling me into his arms. This place that had been my safe place for nearly four years feels wrong.

He loved our baby so much, and I wasn't enough for either of them. I don't deserve to have a baby to love; I struggle to even tolerate myself most days. My mistakes of the past are coming back to haunt me.

"Shh. It's okay."

I shake my head, rubbing snot and tears on Liam's shirt. "No. No. Nothing is okay. I don't deserve to be a mom."

The woman who broke my heart by doing nothing wrong shuffles her feet out of the room after giving us her condolences.

I pull myself from Liam's embrace and sit up, afraid to make eye contact with him. The ultrasound technician hands me a towel to clean myself and a few folded pieces of paper, which, upon inspection, detail what to expect from a miscarriage. The doctor has prescribed me some pills that are supposed to help "expel" our fetus, as if I have banished it from the realm that is my womb. My failure of a uterus that sits dead centre in my failure of a body.

I stand on shaky legs, wanting to void my bladder, but despite the news the man in front of me has delivered, I shouldn't do it on his floor. I excuse myself to go to the bathroom, where I sit on the toilet and cry.

A gentle knock sounds on the door after a while, and I hear Liam on the other side. "Chels, are you okay in there? Can I come in? Are you ready to go home? What can I do?"

He still can't resist asking too many questions at once. I don't have the energy to respond to each one. No, I'm not okay. He can't do anything, and he certainly can't come in.

The best I can do is reply, "I'll be out in a second." I stand, pull my stretchy pants up, shove the papers the man gave me into my shoulder bag, wash my hands, and glare at myself in the mirror. No one who is the descendant of a demon should procreate, anyway.

My self-loathing that I've kept at bay for most of the last four years has taken over my thoughts, and it's very determined. I thought today would be the day I'd see my baby for the first time. Instead, I'm being sent home with pills and a pamphlet about excessive bleeding and cramping. I skimmed over the headings, and beyond the heartbreak, it appears I'm in for a miserable few days.

I open the bathroom door and find the devastated face of my husband. Seeing his upset and disappointment makes the entire scenario worse. How is he ever going to look at me the same way again? I killed his baby. I'm not capable of carrying his children. He can't keep loving me if I am unable to give him the family he wants. What good am I to him?

He says nothing as he pulls me in for a hug. I try to stay composed, but him comforting me makes my already shattered heart turn to dust.

"I love you, Big Red. We'll be okay. I promise."

I want to retort with a snarky comment because he can't promise that. He can't know that for sure. But I know this situation isn't his fault. It's mine. I'm the only one to blame.

I thought when we arrived home to our beautiful, two-story, five-bedroom home set on a bucolic street between Bracebridge and Gravenhurst that we'd be calling our families over for dinner to celebrate. Instead, we're walking inside, not knowing what to say to each other, and allowing the emotional wound to open between us.

How do couples stitch this back together? Do things ever feel right again, or is it just a memory that hangs over your head so in every family photo and vacation you wonder who it is that's missing?

I want my baby back.

I Got Your Back

4

Liam places a plate of sliced fruit in front of me, but it only reminds me that our baby will never ask me for a snack I lovingly prepare. "You have to eat something."

I went to work today for my normal shift, as I've been doing for the past two weeks, but I'm now in our king-sized bed with the blankets pulled over me, ready to embrace the weekend.

Since I miscarried, I've systematically shut everyone out; including Liam. I promised myself I wouldn't do this again because last time it had catastrophic results, but I'm so broken-hearted, I can't put the energy into a relationship with anyone. No one aside from Liam knows we lost a baby, so it's not like I have anyone to talk to. As supportive as my husband tries to be, I can't discuss it with him because he lost just as much as I did, yet he has carried on, seemingly unphased.

"I don't want to eat." I place the food on my bedside table and continue reading my book. But of course, in fiction, even the world's most dangerous assassin has a happy family with children waiting for him at home. Rub it in.

"Chels, you've barely eaten since—"

"Stop. Don't. I don't want to talk about it."

"We need to talk about it. I know you're hurting, but isn't it better if you talk to me? Remember, 'When the world gets too heavy, put it on my back'? From our song?"

I glance up at the wall, zeroing in on the graduation gift I gave Liam years ago with lyrics from the same song; *Always*, by *Panic! At The Disco*. The drawing the words are written on was made by my little sister, Isla, whom I've also been harsh with these past few weeks, and she has no idea why.

I'm the worst. I don't deserve any of these people in my life and I was a fool for thinking I ever did. How could I, drug addict and daughter of the most cold-hearted man to walk the earth, ever have the right to get married and live happily ever after? I don't.

"It's fine, Liam. I should have known better than to get my hopes up." I swipe away the tears trickling down my freckled cheeks.

"What do you mean? You heard what the doctor said. It's common, and a lot of women go through it. It's no fault of yours. Even my mom said—"

"Your MOM? Liam? Your mom, what?" I throw the blanket back, preparing myself to storm off because I am furious. The sadness and self-pity I was feeling have been relegated to the back of my mind.

Liam looks at the cream-coloured area rug on our bedroom floor. "You wouldn't talk to me, and I needed to—"

"Are you kidding me? I didn't want to tell anyone. I don't want everyone else knowing I'm a total failure as a woman. It's bad enough *you* know that."

"You're not a fail—"

"Please, stop." I'm so upset with him for telling his mother. She's going to think less of me than she already does, and I'll never have her approval. I've spent the last four years trying to

17

prove to her I was worthy of her son. I continued with my therapy after rehab, graduated college, got a job working in a drug and addiction counselling office that focuses on prevention and early intervention, and I try my best to be a good wife. Not being able to give her grandchildren is going to make her hate me. Liam is her only child, and therefore, her only chance at grandkids.

"Please, listen to me." He looks at me, waiting for my concession, so I nod. "I told my mom, yes, and I'm sorry for going behind your back. I didn't know how to move forward with pregnancy loss, and I wasn't sure how to help you."

"It wasn't a *pregnancy* loss. It was a baby loss. I couldn't keep our baby alive."

His corners of his full lips droop and he exhales. "Let me finish, please."

My anger is subsiding, being replaced by guilt, bit by bit.

"She said that miscarriages are common, and it's no fault of yours. Once your body heals, there's no reason we can't try again."

I still don't understand how he can move on so easily. It's as though he didn't grieve the loss of our unknown baby at all. For me, moving on is difficult and I don't know if or when I will. "I can't ignore the fact our baby existed. I can't just get over it. And I *can't* just try again. What if it happens again?"

Liam slides into the bed beside me, sweeping his left arm under my head and pulling me into his chest. "We'll never forget the baby we lost, but that doesn't mean we can't give our love to another child. I want to have a family with you, Chels. If you're not ready now, then I understand, but please don't shut me out again and let this pull you under."

I crane my neck to look at him. "I'm not going to use again if that's what you're worried about."

"I'm not worried about you using again; I'm worried about you hurting again. I'm worried about you not letting me help." He kisses the top of my head. "I love you so much, Big Red."

"I love you too, Arizona." My tears are still leaking from my eyes, and guilt has taken over 100 per cent of my emotional capacity. He shouldn't have to help me. Especially not when he's suffering the same loss.

After a few moments letting me cry, Liam says, "when you're ready, we can do something special for our baby to say goodbye."

His words are well meaning, but I don't even get a word out before I'm outright sobbing on his shirt. "I'm so sorry. I'm sorry I couldn't give you a good life. I wanted to, so badly," I blubber at our lost child.

After a few moments, Liam's shirt is more snot than cotton, but he holds me, and we cry together over the child we'll never know but will always love.

We discuss some ideas we can do together in honour of our baby, and we decide to write them a letter. It's something to help us grieve the loss, but also to move forward.

"Sugar." When I hear the name we've chosen for our baby, I get choked up all over again as Liam reads the letter aloud. "It doesn't seem fair, but we were never able to meet. You never got the chance to make a difference in the world, but you should know, you made a big difference in ours. We'll never get to experience your first steps, hear your laugh, or swing you by your arms as we walk hand-in-hand, but your impact on us isn't any less because of that. You will always be our first baby; the first addition to our family. Before we knew the pain of losing you, we knew the joy of loving you, and that will stay with us forever. We would have endured anything to have more time with you, but instead we'll hold space for you in our hearts; a space that will never be empty again. We went from the pinnacle of happiness to the depths of despair during your time with us, and we are grateful to you for teaching us how deep love can go. We love you forever, Mom and Dad."

When Liam sets the letter aside, he pulls me back into his arms, and together we cry ourselves to sleep.

Hearty Appetite

5

t's been four months since Liam and I lost Sugar. Aside from his mom, we told no one else, despite Liam's insistence we tell my family. I don't feel it's necessary to upset them for something they can't change. I remember Zara helping her best friend Quinn through a miscarriage between the births of her two sons, and it took a toll on Zara emotionally. It would be selfish of me to throw that on her again.

Each day I'm improving, and while it still hurts just as much, I have learned to process my grief. Liam's mom, Dola, has been a great support, and I'm happy not to throw my emotional recovery square on Liam's shoulders. I thought Dola would hate me for losing her grandchild, but she's reassured me repeatedly I did nothing to cause a miscarriage. Maybe if she says it seventy-three more times, I'll believe her. Probably not.

The weekend is here, and after Liam had to take a trip to Chicago this week, I'm excited for him to come home. I've spent the last few hours cooking to celebrate his arrival. His dad has gone to pick him up from the airport because he knows how anxious the traffic makes me. I really am lucky to have wonderful in-laws. They make up for the horrific biological family I was dealt.

I have twenty minutes to get dinner on the table so it will be ready for Liam. I invited his parents, but they insisted we have a romantic evening alone. Obviously, they aren't aware of my level of romance. Liam's lucky I brushed my hair and put on a clean t-shirt.

I place the pasta, salad, and roasted chicken at the head of the table so Liam and I can sit in the seats opposite each other. Looking at each other while we stuff our faces seems to be the most romantic arrangement.

When the front door opens, I dash to make sure it is, in fact, my husband walking in and not an ill-intentioned stranger. I've had enough criminal interactions in my life to this point. I hope I can have a few more years without adding more to my tally.

A gorgeous, smiling face beams at me from the door with a bag over his shoulder and a carryon suitcase in tow.

I offer no greeting in the form of words; instead, offering a hug and a knee-buckling hello kiss.

"I missed you so much," Liam says as he drops his bag. "It smells good in here."

"I missed you too. I made dinner. Just basic pasta, salad, and I bought you a chicken."

He raises a brow as one corner of his mouth curls upward. "A chicken? Is it dead or alive?"

"Liam. I would have preferred it alive, but I can't trust you to keep it that way. Get comfortable, and we can eat when you're ready."

Moments later, Liam has returned to our open-concept kitchen wearing track pants and the same t-shirt of his I wore to sleep each night he was gone. He is the most beautiful human

WE'RE ALL A LITTLE TIRED

I've ever met, inside and out, and I can't believe he picked me to be his wife.

"Are you ready to eat?" he asks, disrupting my appreciation.

"I'm starving, actually."

He scoops me into his arms to carry me, but he stumbles as he picks me up, setting me back on my feet. Without acknowledging what just happened, he grabs my hand and leads me to the table. "This looks great."

"I don't know how it tastes, but I hope it's edible."

He kisses my temple before taking his seat, and I take mine. I load up my plate with so much pasta, I haven't left room for salad. I'll eat that later, like a refined Italian—even if I'm an Irish-Canadian. Liam gives me a judgemental look, but I dismiss it and dig into my meal. I slaved away for this; I've earned it.

Our dinner conversation is uneventful, with Liam telling me about some client acquisitions and mergers, which I'll never understand, but I gather were successful. That means he'll have to go back to Chicago in the future to handle some more things, but then he shouldn't need to travel for a while. That's a relief because it's hard when he leaves. I hate being without him and I hate being in our house alone.

Sometimes Isla and her German shepherd Bond come to stay with me for a few nights, so Zach and Zara can have time for themselves. Isla is seventeen now, but because of her social anxiety, she doesn't go out much. As a result, aside from me, she only has one friend, Rory—unless we're counting Bond, which Isla definitely would. She's still doing better than me, because she and Liam are my only friends.

I pile up my plate with a second helping of pasta before eating an entire plateful of salad as well. I'm still hungry, but I'm too embarrassed to load any more food on my plate. Liam already gave me a side-eye when I was looking at the chicken. I've been a vegetarian for ten years, but I consider devouring a chicken breast to satisfy my hunger. At least I have dessert to look forward to. I picked up a cheesecake at a bakery on my way home from work because my baking skills leave a lot to be desired. I can't wait to dig into that next.

"You're hungry tonight." Liam smirks. He's probably aware he's treading in dangerous territory by commenting on my appetite.

"Yeah, I guess I was. I burned a lot of calories cooking. Let me go get dessert."

"Don't you want to digest a little, first?"

I stand in front of my chair, staring at him. Wait? For dessert? That's the worst idea I've ever heard. I can't hide my disappointment, but this is supposed to be my way of celebrating his homecoming. "Oh. Sure. I guess. If that's what you want."

"Let's go sit in the family room and watch a movie."

I doubt there are any movies that are as appealing as cheesecake, but I concede.

Liam lies on our navy-blue sectional sofa and pats the space in front of him.

"I can't fit there. I'll fall on the floor."

"I'd never let you fall. Squeeze in. I'll hang on tight."

I believe he wouldn't let me fall. Aside from falling in love with him, he never has. "Fine. But if you drop me, you're sleeping in the guest room."

He chuckles, knowing I would never make him sleep elsewhere. Especially when he's just returned home after four nights away. "Never."

I settle on the couch, allowing Liam to wrap his arm around my torso as he turns on a new action flick, no doubt with loads of car chases and shootouts. Action movies are my preference over romance these days. I don't want to watch couples falling in love and having children, growing into a happy family. It doesn't always happen that way in real life. Not that the bald guy with an eye-patch trying to take over a nuclear submarine and a rag-tag crew of misfits banding together to save the world is realistic, but it's entertaining.

As we're nearing the second half of the movie, my stomach growls, protesting the forced cheesecake delay. I rub my stomach, as if that's going to satiate the beast. I've got a food baby.

Baby.

When did I get my period last?

I pull Liam's arm off me and hop up.

"What's wrong?"

"Nothing. I just have to pee. I'll be back in a few minutes."

Rather than going to the powder room closest to our family room, I walk through our kitchen and living room into our ensuite, where I stashed the pregnancy tests I bought in bulk. I can't get the packaging open on account of my shaking hands. I tear into it with my teeth; I haven't peed on it yet, so it's okay.

The instructions say to wait three minutes, so I try to keep my mind occupied and avoid looking, but when I'm not staring at the potential for new life inside me, I only think of our Sugar.

The experience between last time and now is remarkably different. Last time, the idea scared me, but I was happy. This time those familiar pink lines cause me to sit on the edge of the bathtub and cry.

A gentle knock at the door moments later startles me. "Chels, are you okay in there?"

I rush to hide the pregnancy test, not wanting Liam to know the result. "My stomach is upset, but I'll be out in a minute."

"Can I get you anything? Maybe you ate too much."

Fine line, Liam. That's a very fine line you are treading.

I splash some water on my face to hide my tears, give myself a final look in the mirror and exit the bathroom, trying my best to pretend I haven't just had my world rocked.

"I guess this means I'm not getting lucky tonight?" He flashes me a cheeky grin, trying to pass his comment off as a joke, but I know he's serious.

"That's not likely, I'm afraid." Crawling into bed, I pull the covers up to my neck and try to think about anything other than the fear regarding those two pink lines I'm experiencing. I feel like a monster for being terrified, but I can't bring myself to get excited, or become attached. What if I lose this baby too? What if my body just isn't cut out for having babies?

Liam crawls in the bed behind me, abandoning our movie. He knows me too well for me to hide the fact something is wrong, but he doesn't press the issue. He sweeps my hair behind my ear, places a gentle kiss on my cheek, and holds me tight like I'm his precious little spoon. I can't bring myself to break his heart again.

Don't
Ovary-act

6

Tonight is our second wedding anniversary and seven whole days since I discovered I am pregnant again. The reality is so terrifying, I have yet to tell Liam. It feels unfair keeping it from him, but I can't bear to disappoint him again. I want to have my first ultrasound before I let him get his hopes up. My appointment is in five weeks, though, so it will be difficult keeping a secret for that long.

My appetite is ravenous, and I want to do everything I can to keep this baby healthy, but I've been so nauseous, stuffing my face on the regular is not enjoyable. My energy level is low, and all of my clothes are tight. The winter weather is working for my benefit because I can wear leggings and sweaters to my job most days.

After a long day at work today, I don't have the energy to make an anniversary-worthy dinner, so we're going to order some food to eat at home. I don't want to get dressed up to go out either, which was Liam's initial suggestion. He probably assumes I wanted to stay home so he can get lucky, but he will be *really* lucky if that happens. My appetite has taken over the space my sex drive once occupied.

To my surprise, when I pull into the garage at the end of our driveway, Liam is already home. Walking through our mudroom, past the powder room and into our kitchen, I look to my right and see Liam already set the dining table. Candles are lit and food containers from the local Thai restaurant I love are open between our wedding dishes we reserve for special occasions.

"Liam?"

The last thing I expect is for Liam to stride out of our bedroom in his boxer shorts, but sure enough, that's what happens. I don't know if I caught him right out of the shower, or if this is an intentional outfit, but I'm not arguing.

"Hey, Big Red." He stops his trek toward me, leaning against the back of our ivory living room sofa, ankles and arms crossed.

"That's a nice outfit you have on, Mr. Davis. Care to explain?"

"I thought it was self-explanatory. I figured we could work up an appetite before having dinner." His devilish grin makes his intentions clear. "All your favourites," he adds with a wink.

I feel so guilty for keeping this massive secret from him, but my life has been fuelled by one upset after the next and every time something good happens, twenty bad things seem to follow. I can't bring myself to hurt him again, but that doesn't make the decision easy. Secret keeping is also a major block to intimacy.

"Liam. Would you hate me if I said I just wanted to eat and have a relaxing night?" The words spill out of my mouth, and I hate *myself* for them, so I won't blame him if he says yes. Is that how things work once children are in the picture? Spousal relationships are sacrificed on account of the kids? Are parents forever too tired after dealing with diapers, tantrums, and bedtime stories to give time and attention to each other? I don't want that for us. I want children—I want a family with Liam. But finding a balance between marriage and parenthood is something we'll have to work on.

"Chels." He strides forward a few paces, settling in front of me. "I'm begging. I'm getting less action than a white crayon." His eye contact wavers as he looks to my left, and the confidence he initially displayed has fled. "I thought we could start trying to get pregnant again. It's been nearly five months, and what better day to start than our anniversary?"

I'm distracted by his crayon comparison because I used to love writing secret messages with white crayons as a kid. Now I'm keeping the biggest secret of all. I really want to tell him, but I'm conflicted. I want to protect him until I know the baby is safe. It's only a few weeks. He'll understand.

While I'm lost in my thoughts, he pulls me into an embrace. In his arms is my safe place, even if he holds more potential to hurt me than anyone—he holds my heart.

"Tell me what's wrong. Please. I can tell there's something bothering you, and I want to help. Are you not ready to try again? We don't have to if you're not ready."

He's being so understanding and accommodating.

Looking at his dark eyes, I see circles underneath that tell me he's tired. Liam tries to protect me from things that stress him too, but we should have figured out by now that we're stronger together. I take a deep exhale. "I'm pregnant."

I blew it again.

Releasing me from his hold, he leans me back to look at my face. "What? How do you know? How long have you known? Are you feeling okay?"

The tears are rolling down my cheeks without permission. I want to celebrate this with him, but I'm so afraid. My fears and concerns start pouring out of me, with no stopping until I've unloaded each one on my wide-mouthed husband.

"Wow. I'm not mad at you for keeping it from me, but I am a little upset. We created this life together, and I want to go through it all with you, Chels. The ups and the downs. So, I understand where you're coming from, but the first thing I need you to promise me is that you won't keep anything like this from me again."

Shame washes over me and I feel terrible for not realizing that. It wasn't fair for me to take the joy and excitement from him. I've made a lot of strides in healing from my traumas, but some habits are hard to break. My instincts have spent over two decades training me to avoid upsetting people at all costs in hopes they'll love me. The stupid thing is, Liam has never given me reason to doubt his love. Logically, I know he's all in. I know he's not my father. He loves me, and I *know* that.

I nod.

"It will be okay. We'll go to your appointment in a few weeks, and this time I bet we'll have a strong, healthy baby. Until then, we'll just make sure that you eat well and get your vitamins." Panic spreads across Liam's face. "Have you been taking vitamins?"

"Yes. I've been taking them since before we got pregnant last time, but they didn't help then."

"Don't worry. We'll take one day at a time and do everything we can to give our baby the best life possible. Do you know how far along you are?" Liam is holding me tight against his scantily clad body, unphased by his lack of attire.

Looking away from his face, I say, "I think about five or six weeks. Give or take. My cycle has always been irregular, so it didn't occur to me until last week."

Liam walks around sofa, collapsing into a corner seat. "Wow. And they can't get you in sooner for an ultrasound?"

"I asked, but they don't recommend it unless I have issues. I even had to beg to get one at all before twelve weeks."

He stares blankly at the abstract art piece hung above our fireplace. "I'm happy."

His admission feels so random and out of place in our conversation, so I take a second to register his words. "Yeah? You're okay with this? Despite the risks? I mean, we could lose another baby, and I'm not sure I can handle that."

"I know there's a chance, but it's a small one. No risk, no reward. If we keep living in fear of losing another baby, we may never get the chance to hold one in our arms. So, yeah. I'm happy there's a chance we'll have a little baby running around soon."

I giggle. "It's not going to come out running. That will hopefully take a year or so."

He reaches up, grabbing my hand and pulling me over the back of the sofa onto his lap. I land with an "*oomph*."

"I'm so sorry. Are you okay? Did I hurt you? Did I hurt the baby?"

"Liam. Calm down. You just surprised me. We're fine as far as I can tell."

The weight of those words hangs in the air over us both. I felt like everything was fine last time, too.

We spend our anniversary, not entangled in sheets, or each other. Instead, we talk about people we dislike and would never name our child after—ahem, Kevin, Sebastian, and Gia are all hard nos. We pick which bedroom we'll convert into a nursery, and research family vehicles that have the best safety ratings. A decidedly unromantic evening, but romance isn't always the goal. Tonight we talked about our future as a family, and that means a lot more to me than candles and flowers.

Skip a Beat

7

I've impatiently waited for my first ultrasound appointment to arrive for the last several weeks. Each day has dragged as if someone set time to play at half-speed, but today is finally the day. Liam booked the afternoon off work so he can attend the appointment with me. I know in his mind, he wants to be there for the good news, but in mine, I'm happy to have him there in the event of bad news again.

My pregnancy has been uneventful aside from the nausea and indigestion plaguing my existence. This child has been tormenting me since conception, and I can only hope the life it's zapping from me is keeping it strong and healthy. Continuing to work has been difficult because I don't want to tell anyone I am expecting yet, and my regular trips to the bathroom have become a hot topic for office gossip among the seven employees.

I've adjusted my schedule to have today off, and in turn I will work Saturday. It's not my favourite, because then I miss out on a day with Liam over the weekend, but I knew I wouldn't be in any place mentally to be productive at work today. I get myself ready in stretchy cotton leggings and an oversized sweater to accommodate my belly. It's not obvious, by any means, but it's enough of a difference, jeans are not an option.

I drive to the diagnostic centre where we'll be anxiously awaiting news of our baby's current condition, and stand outside the main lobby, awaiting my husband's arrival from work.

Liam pulls into the parking lot in his black Infiniti Q50, which he upgraded to after his first full year in his job. I relax knowing he's going to be by my side when we receive the answers we've been anticipating for weeks. He parks directly beside my seven-year-old, second-hand, white Kia Sorento. I have no desire to upgrade because I don't make a lot of money at my job, and I don't want Liam paying for every big-ticket item we purchase.

My beautiful man walks toward me in his charcoal grey business suit, black shoes and a black wool car coat, which he's left unbuttoned. The smile he sends my way before leaning in for a kiss is exactly what I need right now. I wrap my arms around him, feeling his warmth, and enjoying the safety of his embrace for a brief moment.

"Are you ready?"

Without letting go of him, I reply, "yes and no." Spending most of my life with my fight-or-flight mode constantly activated, it really serves no purpose here. There's nothing I can do to guarantee survival—certainly not survival for our baby.

"I know." He eases my head onto his shoulder, pulling me in tighter. "Let's just go in and see what they have to say before we worry, yeah?"

This man is speaking to me as if my worry is some logical being I can rationalize with. In reality, my anxious thoughts operate with the same level of practicality as a toddler three hours past naptime. "Right. I'll *wait* to panic. That makes much more sense."

Liam chuckles, understanding my sarcastic tone, and leads me by the hand inside, out of the cool air characteristic of Bracebridge in late March.

I register with the receptionist while Liam stands dutifully at my side, rubbing gentle circles with his thumb on my lower back. The sensation is subtle, but it's enough to distract my mind from the unknowns we're facing.

As we sit in the reception area, my emotions are a stark contrast to the last time we were here. At that time, I waited with excitement, wonder, and hope. Today, my anxiety level is increasing exponentially with each minute we're left waiting. Not to mention, my bladder is protesting every deep inhale, and I'm praying I don't cough or sneeze.

"Are you okay?" Liam reaches to take my hand in his.

"Yeah. Just nervous. Last time—"

"Every pregnancy is different. I know it's tough to move on, but just because it happened once doesn't mean it will happen again," he interrupts, giving me a squeeze of my hand.

I take a steadying breath, nodding and willing my tears not to spill out right as the ultrasound technician calls my name.

"It's going to be fine, Chels. Whatever they tell us, we're going to be okay." Liam stands, extending a hand to help me up as if I'm more like nine months pregnant than nine weeks. "Let's do this."

Again, I'm instructed to remove the clothing from my top half and put on a polyester hospital gown before entering the exam room. Liam is seated at the head of the examination table, leg bouncing as he rubs his hands along his thighs. He's probably trying to resist asking the fifty questions he has in his mind.

The ultrasound technician is a woman this time, and she introduces herself as Alyssa. She has beautiful bright blue eyes and pale skin, much like my own, and long, pin-straight, dark blonde hair. I'm more at ease than I was last time, despite my fears. When the offensive gel squirts onto my lower abdomen and Alyssa moves the contraption around, her unreadable expression turns to one of concern.

"Is everything okay?" My heart sinks.

"It just takes a few moments to find what I'm looking for. Just breathe steadily and try to keep still." She smiles at me, but she's displaying the same fake smile I implemented for nearly two decades. That's not a happy smile.

I lie there, trying to choke back my impending tears, when she flicks on the computer's sound and I hear the steady, rapid heartbeat of our unborn baby. Tears of relief spring from my eyes, and Liam leans down to kiss my forehead.

Alyssa still says nothing as she continues to move the probing device in a small area of skin, tilting it in every direction, typing randomly and taking still shots I am hoping we'll be able to take home later today.

"I'll be right back, okay?" Alyssa stands from her stool and exits the room without waiting for a reply.

My earlier relief evaporates and I'm terrified all over again. Liam does his best to comfort me, reminding me we heard the baby's heartbeat, but I can't help wondering what else could justify leaving the room other than if something is wrong with our baby and she needs a second opinion.

Five minutes later, Alyssa returns and instructs me to remove the clothing from my bottom half so she can do a transvaginal ultrasound. I am not entirely sure what that is because Liam and his mother have banned me from searching pregnancy forums, but if I have to take my pants off and it includes the word "vaginal," I'm fairly certain it's going to be awkward.

Yep, it's awkward. I keep telling myself to relax, but that's incredibly difficult when you're laying spread eagle in front of a stranger and she has an eight-inch curling-iron thing wearing a condom stuffed up your bajingo. Do not recommend. Liam appears even more traumatized than I am, and to ease the tension in typical Chelsea fashion, I up the awkward ante. "What's the male version of this machine look like?"

Without batting an eye, Alyssa replies, "typically, if we aren't able to get photos with a transabdominal ultrasound, we would require a transrectal—"

"That's super interesting." Liam cuts in, glaring at me. "What can you tell us about the baby? Does everything look okay?"

"I'm still trying to get the images I need. She's still quite early along, so it can be tricky sometimes."

Alyssa carries on, doing what she's doing, snapping pictures of my downstairs, and her face now appears content. I'm not sure if she's got a wicked poker face, or if she is genuinely happy about what she is seeing. I tell myself she does this several times a day, so seeing little baby beans is nothing new for her. What she may not realize is that I'm dying to see our baby on that screen.

This procedure is taking decades—at least, it feels that way. I do my best to lie still, breathe normally, move as requested, and hold my breath on command. Each passing moment makes my bladder scream a little louder. When Alyssa finally removes the transducer—the fancy term for the contraption that spent the last thirty minutes getting to know me more intimately than I ever could have wanted—I immediately close my legs as if I have any modesty left.

"Well, I've got all the necessary images." She's avoiding eye contact with Liam and me, which is not easing my anxieties. "This is your first ultrasound, correct?"

Her question hits me like a slap in the face. "First one for this pregnancy, yes."

"Well, I have some exciting news for you."

Womb and Board

8

I beg your pardon? Am I having an out-of-body moment right now? Is this another nightmare? Triplets? As in three babies. "There are three babies growing inside of me? Are you sure I don't have a couple of tumours or something? How sure are you?"

Alyssa giggles. "I'm 100% sure there are three babies in there, yes."

I look at Liam, look at Alyssa, and try my best not to panic-vomit on the floor, knowing I'd probably pee myself in the process. Liam looks white as a ghost—a remarkable feat for his caramel complexion. This may be the first time in all the years we've known each other that I've seen him speechless and unable to offer words of comfort to me.

This time, it's my turn to be the strong one. Pulling myself together, I reach a hand to his arm. "Liam. Are you okay?"

He issues a silent nod without blinking his eyes. He's staring directly forward at the screen depicting three bean-like objects in a grainy black-and-white image. The letters A, B, and C show the three humans who have been secretly growing inside me for the past ten weeks. It's no wonder I've felt so sick. And hungry. And tired!

"I've forwarded the information on to your doctor, and I'd recommend you make an appointment within the next few days to discuss the results."

"Right. Sure. Of course. Thank you." I swing my legs over the edge of the exam table, looking at my husband. "Liam? Are you ready to go?" He doesn't acknowledge me, still staring blankly at the image. I look at Alyssa with pleading eyes.

"Let me print out a few pictures for you to take with you." She turns the screen away from Liam, finally breaking his focus.

"Are you going to be all right?" I tilt my head, curious if he's lost his ability to speak.

"Th... three... three babies? Three? How... but how?"

Well, he's not mute, but he seems to have suffered some type of shock-induced aphasia. "Come on. I'm going to get changed and go to the bathroom. We can talk about this in a few minutes." I'm sure there are other patients waiting for their appointments and I'm eager to dehydrate myself.

Liam eases to stand, creeping forward like a tentative toddler. I am already carrying three extra bodies; I am not carrying my grown husband who is nearly double my size. What if his children are gigantic? I have to ask Dola how much Liam weighed at birth, because I don't think my frame can sustain a little football team.

Once I've changed and used the washroom, Liam is on the phone with my doctor's office arranging an appointment to discuss my ultrasound results. I have so many questions. Do I need to take three multi-vitamins for three babies? What should my daily calorie intake be? Lost in my world of unanswered questions, a voice stops us before we reach the door.

38

"Mrs. Davis?"

I spin around, still unfamiliar with being called that after two years of marriage. "Yes?"

"Your photos." The petite brunette receptionist with coffee-coloured skin hands me a strip of shiny, three by five photos. I nod my thanks and stand in the middle of the waiting room, gawking at the reality that is my womb.

I notice the white lettering at the top says 'EDD: OCT 13'. I'm not sure what that means. We didn't receive any photos last time, so this is a new step for us. I turn back to ask the receptionist, "what does 'EDD' mean?"

"Oh, that's your estimated due date."

"Thank you." October 13. That's just shy of seven months away. Seven months and we *could* have three babies to care for. Seven months until we *could* be a family of five. But I'm really afraid to get my hopes up and plan for that. Life laughs at my plans.

Just as I'm spiralling into complete overwhelm, Liam walks toward me, placing an arm around my back. "Can I see?" I stretch the strip of photos for him to examine each one. "Wow. Those are our babies." He leans in, kissing my jaw below my ear.

"Our babies."

Our drive home in separate vehicles allows us each time to process today's news before we talk about it together. I arrive home first, parking in our garage and going inside to wait for Liam. I'm not even sure how to have this conversation. What will come of discussing the bombshell dropped on us today? I'm terrified, shocked, and maybe a little excited.

Liam and I were both only children—at least, I didn't know about my brother until my early twenties and don't wish to see him ever again. The idea of our kids growing up with automatic best friends is nice to think about.

After forty-five minutes, Liam still isn't home and I worry he's run off because he's afraid of what's coming. Before I allow myself more time to doubt my husband's integrity, I walk into our bedroom to change into something more comfortable. Yes, more comfortable than cotton leggings and an oversized sweater.

Liam walks into our bedroom as I'm changing and his eyes light up like Times Square. "Today must be my lucky day." He strides across the room as I rush to pull his ratty grey t-shirt over my head.

"Liam, no. The babies."

His eyes shift from side to side as if he's searching our bedroom for watching children. "What about the babies?"

I narrow my eyebrows enough I can feel the wrinkles form on my forehead. "What if you hurt them?"

"Chels. Pregnant people are allowed to have sex. I'm pretty sure it's recommended."

"I'm not a normal pregnant woman, Liam. There are three babies in here! Three! I couldn't even keep one baby alive. What makes you think I'll be able to keep three?" It doesn't matter how much Liam or his mom tells me every pregnancy is different, or how much reassurance I get from looking at these grainy black and white photos. I am going to worry about these babies every moment until I hold them in my arms. Then I'll worry about them still, until my dying breath.

"I know it's scary. I just about passed out, so it terrifies me too..." He laughs at himself. "But I don't want us to grow apart."

"So, sex is the only thing keeping us together? If I don't provide that on a whim, then we're bound to be calling some skeezy divorce lawyer from a bus stop bench?"

He gives me his 'are you serious' face. "You know that's not what I'm saying. It's not the only thing keeping us together, obviously. But I can't deny that few things make me happier than getting lost in you. In us."

I know I shouldn't doubt Liam or his intentions, but *I* can't deny that I'm scared. When I feel fearful, I push people away. I've realized this habit through countless rounds of therapy, and I've learned to recognize it before I spiral too far. Hopefully. "I'm just scared. Can we wait until I have my next doctor's appointment? I need some more reassurance. I don't want to take any chances."

Liam sighs but leans in to give me a chaste kiss, handing me a box of chocolates. They're from a place about twenty minutes away called *Chelsea's Chocolates*, and he knows they're my favourite. "Of course. I don't want you doing anything you're not comfortable with. I guess I'll settle for a few of your chocolates." He leans in so his breath blows across my ear as he speaks. "But just so you know, you look so sexy carrying my babies."

A shiver runs through me, but that only sets off alarm bells in my bladder that have begun to dictate my life. I rush off to the bathroom, leaving Liam standing in our room like a dejected teenage boy. The only difference: Liam is all man.

When I emerge, he's sitting on the edge of the bed holding a creased piece of paper. I immediately recognize it and move to sit beside him. He places his comforting arm around me as I lean into him, staring at the letter we wrote our lost baby.

"Look." Liam points to the top of the letter.

October 13.

I take a second to understand the significance. Our due date is exactly one year from the day we said our final goodbye to Sugar. My emotions threaten to pour out, but I fight to keep them at bay, not wanting Liam to feel the need to comfort me again. When I look at Liam and notice he has tears running down his cheeks, I can't contain my own. We sit in our room, wrapped in each other's arms, releasing a combination of joy and sorrow. Joy for what's to come, and sorrow for what we lost.

It takes Guts

9

Liam was able to get me scheduled in with my family physician the Tuesday after my ultrasound. The fact that his mother is a well-respected physician in the area is not something he was afraid to mention when they initially said it would be two weeks before they could squeeze me in. Unfortunately, Liam couldn't take another day off, so here I am, sitting in the stark waiting room, surrounded by strangers and cheap vinyl furniture. I'm playing with my phone to distract myself, eager to see Dr. Rowe for the first time since my follow-up appointment after losing Sugar.

"Chelsea Davis," a fellow ginger calls from the entrance to the hallway leading to the exam rooms.

I shove my phone into my shoulder bag, rushing off behind the woman who looks like she could be related to me. Given that I had a brother I knew nothing about, it's not something I can assume isn't true.

"Take a seat in here and the doctor will be with you shortly."

Oh yay. Now I can sit in *here* and be anxious. I read every word on the 'Dangers of Smoking' poster, as well as the labelled diagram depicting a human's ear, nose, and throat. I consider myself an expert by the time Dr. Charles Rowe enters the room.

"Hi, Chelsea. I gather you've gotten some exciting news since I saw you last." He has a faint British accent, having been born in the UK and emigrating to Canada as a teen. His white hair and weathered hands betray his age, which I'd estimate to be around sixty. He's old school. No nonsense.

I sit on the exam table, picking at my fingernails as I reply, "you can say that again." Releasing a deep exhale, I try to breathe out some of my worries, but my stomach is a ball of nerves.

"I see here the ultrasound estimates your due date around October 13th, and from what they could tell, all three babies look fine so far, but it is early."

Repeating my due date in my head, I reassure myself everything will be fine. "Okay. We have seven months to plan for them, right? To figure out what we're going to do? It scared me to have one child; but three?" I rattle off my thoughts and, in just a matter of words, my convincing has been undone.

"Actually, you're past ten weeks, and triplets are born prematurely, so I'd say you have more like five months... or less."

I look at Dr. Rowe with wide eyes, noticing his gritted teeth. "I'm sorry? Five? As in one hand? I'm supposed to have three children in five months? I have five months to grow three fully formed human beings?" The enormity of the task ahead of me, over not just the next five months, but eighteen-plus years, is a lot to process.

"Well, Chelsea, something you might want to consider is selective reduction."

43

I don't like the sound of that. "What is 'selective reduction?'"

"We can choose one or two of the embryos that look healthiest and stand the best chance of survival and eliminate the others."

Did I hear that correctly? "I'm sorry. Did you just say you want me to choose which of my babies lives and which dies? Is that really what you're suggesting?"

"It's not quite so simple. We do tests to determine which are most likely to survive."

I think I understand the grizzly mom mode that I teased Zara about for years, because I feel it now. "Doctor, first of all, they are not 'which', they are 'who'. Second, in your years of your practice, have you ever been wrong?"

His brows furrow. "Yes. Unfortunately, medicine isn't an exact science, but we do our best."

"Right, and you're asking me to choose which one of my babies has a chance at life based on your flawed science?"

"It is highly accurate, Mrs. Davis. It's not a shot in the dark."

"I respectfully disagree, Dr. Rowe. No one will be *reducing* my babies. I will assume all risks to myself, and them, but they are all getting a chance to live."

"Mrs. Davis, perhaps you should discuss the option with your husband before making a final decision. Here's a pamphlet for you to look through on the risks of multiples births, so you can make a more informed decision."

The audacity of this man.

"I'm well enough informed, thank you. Thank you for your time, doctor." I grab my coat and storm out of his office, ready to put some distance in between myself and the man suggesting I eliminate my unborn children. When we lost Sugar, I felt a pain I didn't know possible. Choosing to do that on purpose? No. It's not an option. I don't care what science says.

WE'RE ALL A LITTLE TIRED

When I arrive home, I call Liam to relay the information from my appointment. As I expected, he is outraged, maybe even more so than me.

"Should I call my mom and ask what she thinks? Not about the reduction, but about the doctor? Maybe he isn't the right one for us, Chels. I know you went to him because you were in a pinch, but we can look elsewhere."

I lean back on the couch, kicking my feet up onto our rustic coffee table, careful to avoid the vase of fake flowers in the centre. It occurs to me with three kids around, things like that are going to have to find a new home. "I'll be referred to an obstetrician soon, so I don't have to deal with him for long. I just feel better knowing you agree with me and have my back."

"Always. You know that."

I do know that. He's always my voice of reason when I'm teetering on the edge of a breakdown. He's my sounding board when I need to hash out the hundreds of nonsensical feelings bouncing around my head. He's my rock when I need support and strength. So knowing he agrees with me on this issue confirms my decision was justified.

"I do. I'll make something for dinner and we can talk when you get home. Sorry for bugging you at work. That was just outrageous, and I needed to vent."

"You never bother me. Ever. And I'm glad you called. Hearing your voice makes a long day at the office more tolerable. I'll be home soon. I love you."

"I love you too."

After a few moments to decompress from this morning's events, trying to wrap my head around having five months to prepare for our population explosion, I finally relax. Beyond that, I know Dr. Rowe was just sharing what he felt was a reasonable option, and I wouldn't judge anyone who went that route, but I can't. I could never look one of our children in the eye, say "I love you" to them, knowing my decision could have just as easily ended their life.

My mind is made up, and I'll do whatever I can to give all three babies happy, healthy lives. Even if that means gaining eighty pounds, and having my guts rearranged to pull them out of my body.

Now is a good time to look up some information on multiples c-sections online.

Whaaa... Why? I knew I shouldn't have done that. I *knew* I shouldn't have done that. Liam is always telling me not to consult Dr. Google and look at what I went and did. Note, do not look at C-section photos, nor read C-section horror stories when you know one is in your near future.

"Chels?"

I frantically stuff my phone in the couch cushions like I'm having an illicit affair. Me and Google have been quite intimate over the last few hours.

"Hey, what are you doing?" Liam's concerned eyes meet mine as I spin around on the sofa to face him.

"Oh, hey. I didn't realize it was so late. I haven't made dinner yet."

Sitting down beside me, he leans over to give me a kiss, and it doesn't escape my notice that our house isn't a home until he's in it. "That's okay. Were you having a nap?"

I consider lying and saying I was, but I can't do that to him. My face would give me away in an instant, anyway. "Uh. No. I was reading some stuff online."

Liam huffs out a grumble. "Chelsea. What were you reading online?"

"I was reading about c-sections for multiples births, and pregnancy stories." Liam tries to say something, but I continue,

46

"I just wanted to have some insight about what to expect, but it was a terrible mistake because what I read… what I *saw*… well, it was horrific. I don't know if I can do this."

He pulls me toward him, chuckling, and the sound makes my stress level go from 3,000 to fifty in a heartbeat. "How many times do I have to tell you not to look up medical stuff online? It never turns out well."

He's right.

"I know; I was curious, and since no one in our families knows yet, I didn't have anyone else to talk to about it. It's not like I can call you at work and bother you all day. I just—"

"I get it. I was googling things because I feel a little unprepared too. But maybe try sticking to looking up things like which diapers are best, or which cribs have the best safety ratings, yeah?"

"Yeah. Okay. What did you look up?"

Liam's eyebrows nearly merge into his perfectly shaped hairline. "You don't want to know."

Going Viral

10

'm officially twelve weeks pregnant. We've made it through what's considered the "danger zone" with a normal pregnancy, but with triplets, the entire pregnancy is a danger zone.

We've decided to have our families over to share the news, so Liam bought me a t-shirt to wear, and we'll see how long it takes everyone to figure it out. I'm wearing a cardigan overtop, but pregnancy hormones are no joke because I feel like *I* am a bun in an oven, so I don't know how long I'll be able to keep it on.

Zara, Zach, and Isla are the first to arrive. I love my family so much, and honestly, after everything I've put them through, they would have been justified in dismissing me and never speaking to me again, but they couldn't have been more supportive. I know they'll be excited about the babies.

"Hi. Thanks for coming." As they walk through the door, I hug them each, starting with Zach. I've made a conscious effort the past few years to be more affectionate toward those I love, and the change hasn't gone unnoticed. The man before me with dirty-blond hair, striking green eyes and a permanent five o'clock shadow is the first man who never disappointed me. He never hurt me. He loved me even when I would have understood if he didn't. A simple hug can never convey that, but I'll keep trying.

Zara's medium-brown hair is pulled back into a loose bun allowing me to see her smile ear to ear. At nearly forty, she still could pass for my sister, but the smile lines around her deep-green eyes have become more prominent. The fact she's smiled enough to develop those faint wrinkles makes me beam in return. "Hi Sweetheart. Thanks for having us."

Isla hands me a casserole dish in an insulated floral bag. I can tell from the smell that it's Zara's vegetable lasagna. "Hi Chels. Mom made this."

"Thanks Troublemaker. And thanks, Mom."

It still amazes me how much her face lights up when I say that.

As everyone makes their way inside, I notice Liam's parents, Ian and Dola, pulling into our driveway. Liam is chatting with Zach, but I holler at him to come welcome his parents and make my way to place the lasagna in the kitchen before coming back to greet my in-laws.

I don't know what everyone complains about with in-laws, because I couldn't have asked for anyone better. Liam certainly didn't fare very well in that department if we're counting my biological family, but Zach, Zara and Isla are wonderful. Having grown up with no relatives at all most of my life, I can say now I have one big, happy family, and I love each of them.

When Liam opens the door, letting in a welcomed cool April breeze, his parents' smiling faces are waiting on the other side. His mother's beautiful mocha skin is glowing under the spring sun, and she's dressed in a coral-coloured skirt suit. She looks stunning.

I greet Ian first; his facial stubble brushing my cheek as he leans in to give me a hug. Liam's dad is the kind of man who other men should look up to. He shares an Irish heritage with my own father, but that's where their similarities end. He's kind, intelligent, hardworking, and he loves his family more than anything. He had a heart attack several years ago, so his doctor-wife has had him on a strict diet regimen ever since in order to prolong his life as much as possible. He is the picture of health today.

When Liam and I trade places so he can welcome his father, his mother eyes me skeptically. She smirks, and I feel like a child who was caught with her hand in the cookie jar. She knows about our miscarriage last year, so she has every right to be apprehensive why we've invited everyone over. I hoped the fact it's Liam's birthday would make everyone assume we were having a dinner for him, but we've never made a big deal of birthdays in the past, so it is suspicious and Dola is not one to miss an abnormality of any sort. Oblivious is not a word I'd use to describe her.

"Hi, Love. How are you?" Dola greets me with a peck and a tight squeeze.

"I'm good, thank you. You look beautiful."

She smiles at me again, but it's not strictly a cheerful smile. She's smiling like she knows something.

Now that everyone is here, I busy myself in the kitchen, trying to prepare the food so it will be ready at the same time. Liam has set the table, and he's entertaining Zach, Zara, Ian, and Dola in the family room to the left of our kitchen, while Isla helps me with food prep. I've missed my little sister, and though this isn't a relaxing hangout, I'm happy to spend time with her.

"How's school?"

"I'm done."

I nearly drop the dish of potatoes I'm holding. "What? You're done? What do you mean you're done?"

"I finished. I was ahead in my classes, and because they were all online, I finished early... like two months ago."

"Done the semester?"

"No. Done, done. Finished. Finito."

I stare at her while I internally beat myself up for not knowing that she was on the verge of finishing high school. Have I been so distracted with my own life that I've neglected basic sisterly duties? "Isla. Wow. That's amazing. Why didn't you tell me? We should have had a graduation party or something."

She laughs. "Who would we invite, Chels? Bond and Rory? That's basically what I did, anyway."

I can't help but feel a little hurt that she had a celebration and didn't think to even tell me. This is what I get for pushing her away when I miscarried; cut out of big life events.

My face must give away my disappointment because Isla reaches a hand over to my arm. "I could tell you had a lot on your mind, and I didn't think it was a big deal, so I was just waiting to tell you."

"It is a big deal, Isla. It's huge. Finishing high school and moving on to the next phase of your life is a major accomplishment. I wish I could have celebrated that with you." I give her a wry smile because I don't want her to think I'm upset with her. It's myself I'm upset with for being a lousy sister. "What are your plans now?"

She smiles back and we have an understanding pass between us. "I'm taking a few months off until college starts in the fall. I've been working on my writing and looking to find work as a freelance copywriter or something."

Isla is an incredibly talented writer, and I have no doubts she'll be a best-selling author one day. It keeps me in line as a sister, because I don't want to end up killed off in one of her future books.

51

Liam walks in the room with a smirk on his face. "Do you need any help?"

"Everything is ready, so you can help carry stuff to the table."

He darts around the island, giving me a kiss before grabbing a couple of dishes and making his way to the dining room. When he comes back for a second load, he asks, "aren't you feeling hot?" He gives me a playful wink.

It's so hot in here; I want nothing more than to rip this cardigan off. Trying to make it seem casual and not draw attention, I grab a bowl of salad, walk into the dining room, remove my sweater and place it over the back of a chair. When I walk back into our kitchen, toward the family room, Isla spots my t-shirt.

"Our first litter? That's a weird shirt, Chels."

I laugh because she hasn't caught on. Liam thought it was clever, and he thinks he's hilarious, so I played along.

"Dinner is served, everyone," Liam calls to our guests.

Everyone turns to look at us standing in the room's entryway, and Dola shouts, "I knew it! Wait. Litter?" Her accent says the word litter in the most beautiful way. I could listen to her forever. Perfectly pronounced consonants. I digress.

Liam chuckles, unable to contain himself. He really thinks he's funnier than he is, so I expect a lot of dad jokes in my future.

"You mean there's more than one?" Dola remarks, cluing in to what the shirt implies.

"More than one what?" Ian asks.

"Baby!" Dola replies, shooting him a look that you know could keep anyone in line.

Zara looks like she's about to faint, but instead bursts into tears. She couldn't have children of her own, so for a moment, I'm worried our announcement has made her upset. I rush over to hug her. "Are you okay? Don't be sad."

"Sad? Why would I be sad? Chelsea, this is amazing? Are you really having two babies?"

I grin at her. "No. We're not having two." Looking around the room, everyone seems disappointed by that news, so I clarify. "We're having three."

A collective gasp reverberates through the space. "Three?" Zach asks. "Three babies? Not puppies?"

I laugh. "No, puppies. Yes, babies. Three babies."

"I'm going to be a grandma," Zara adds, realizing what the revelation means.

"Don't worry, Baby. You're still a GILF," Zach adds, which earns him a slap on his chest from Zara, and a collective "ew" from Isla and me.

Zara, Dola, and Isla are all crying happy tears, and pull me into a group hug. The men soon surround us, and at that moment, I feel all the love our babies will be wrapped in.

Liver Little

II

Dola has gotten us a referral to a friend of hers who works at *Mount Sinai* in Toronto, specializing in multiples pregnancies, and I couldn't be more grateful. After the conversation with Dr. Rowe, I expressed my fears and concerns to Dola, and she reassured me she would advocate for the babies and me through this process. She's attending my ultrasound in Toronto with me today and having the one-on-one time with her has been nice. She's clearly excited to become a grandma.

When we arrive at the hospital, like the gem she is, Dola lets me out at the front entrance before making her way into the underground parking. I've made a lot of progress over the last few years, but there are still some things I'd prefer to avoid if given the choice. Underground parking garages are one of those things. When she exits the elevator into the hospital lobby, she moves with such confidence and poise, I can't help but stride along behind her.

We make our way to the ultrasound clinic, and my nerves are soaring right along with the elevator. Dola reaches out and grabs my hand in between both of hers, capturing my attention. "Just breathe, Love. This hospital employs some of the best doctors in the world. I have the utmost faith in them. I wouldn't trust my grandbabies or my daughter to just anyone."

When she calls me her daughter, a lump forms in my throat. I grew up without a mother, but now I'm lucky enough to have two. I know already how much love I have for the children I am growing, but these women love me just the same as if I were their own. They each showed up in my life when I needed them most, but for my own children, I vow to never leave them in need.

"Thank you, Dola. I believe you."

After waiting for thirty-five minutes, I'm finally called in for my ultrasound, which will immediately be sent to the doctor I'll be seeing for the rest of my pregnancy. The fact I don't have to wait days for results is comforting. Also, having Dola by my side makes me infinitely more confident in understanding whatever the doctors tell me. My area of expertise is drug addiction; medical terminology is not my forte.

I lie on the exam table through another uncomfortable ultrasound. My belly is protruding enough I look pregnant, not just bloated. It's exciting to see the growth, because to me, that signals healthy baby growth.

The sonographer, Vanessa, explains that at sixteen weeks, a fetus is the size of an avocado. I imagine my three little avocados hanging out, fluttering around, conspiring what they'll make uncomfortable next. I chuckle at the thought before I glimpse Vanessa's furrowed brows, and Dola's hand clamps onto mine.

My mind goes into panic mode, tears well in my eyes, and I'm struggling to take a deep breath. "Wha... What's wrong?"

"The doctor will discuss the results with you shortly. No need to panic," Vanessa replies without looking my direction.

No need to panic? I'm sorry, Vanessa, but my mind doesn't *need* a reason to panic. It just does. When you're looking at images of my babies with a face like someone's force feeding you a fried tarantula, it's very much a cause for concern.

"Don't worry, Love. We'll see what the doctor has to say. Could you show her the babies? That might put her mind at ease." No one can say no to Dola's do-it-or-else smile.

Vanessa turns the monitor toward me and presses a key to turn on the sound. She shows me baby A, baby B, and baby C. It takes some time to capture them all, but I hear three heartbeats and confirm they are moving around like little jumping avocados. Holy guacamole.

I feel a modicum of relief, but I can't ignore the look she had on her face. When she gives me the go-ahead to wipe the gel off of my abdomen and head to the doctor's office for results, my anxiety comes marching right along with me. I look down at the printed image I purchased so I can take it home for Liam — the best five dollars I've ever spent. Looking at my babies, even though they are barely recognizable as babies, has me flooded with emotions. Love being the primary one, fear being a close second.

When we're called into Dr. Steel's office a short time after arriving to register with the receptionist, I'm having a hard time determining if that's because they're efficient, or because there's urgent news to tell me.

I'm seated on yet another exam table in an office plastered with pregnancy posters, and Dola is in a chair to my left.

When the door opens, a tall, ivory-skinned gentleman with deep blue eyes and an auburn crew cut issues a smile before speaking. "Dola, lovely to see you. How have you been?"

My mother-in-law stands, skipping a handshake, giving the man a hug. "I'm well Harvey. How are you? How are Phoebe and the kids?"

"Phoebe is feeling a bit out of sorts now as an empty nester. The youngest flew the coup last fall."

"Wow, that's hard to believe. I remember when your first was born while we were in med school. Time flies."

"That it does." He takes a seat on his wheeled black-leather stool, setting a manila folder down on the desk and opening a file on his computer.

As he spins around to face me, Dola speaks, "this is my daughter-in-law Chelsea, and my grandbabies. I'm trusting you with giving them the best possible care."

"Nothing but the best for all of my patients." He winks, and his light-hearted nature sets me at ease. "Now, Chelsea, this is your first pregnancy?"

This old wound keeps being reopened, and I never know what to say. Yes? No? "I had a miscarriage last year at eleven weeks."

"I'm sorry to hear that. I know it can add some anxiety with subsequent pregnancies, but even more so when you're carrying three. The ultrasound looks good. Baby A and Baby C are right on track with size and where we'd expect them to be."

"Baby B?" I ask, without letting him finish his sentence.

His sympathetic smile has my fear flooding back in an instant. "Baby B looks fine, but the measurements of the liver are slightly higher than we want them. Now, our ultrasounds are good, but they're not perfect, so that could be the reason for the discrepancy. In order to be sure, we'll take a full family medical history and send you for a detailed fetal ultrasound to get more information. An enlarged liver can be an issue, but like I said, we don't know anything for sure until we get more information, so try your best to keep calm."

Dola is seated on the exam table beside me, right arm around my shoulders and her left hand holding mine. I'm trying to process everything the doctor is telling me, but I don't know where to start.

"Are we able to get that done today, Harvey? Or do we come back?"

"I tried to shuffle some things around because I know it's a long drive for you, but they're at capacity today. I can get you in on Friday at the earliest."

Three days. That's three days to try to continue with my life as normal, knowing one of our babies could have something seriously wrong.

"I'm adopted," I blurt. "I don't have a medical history. All I know are my parent's names and that my father is in a penitentiary in Alberta. Is this..." I choke down my words because I am afraid to know the answer. "Is this because I used drugs before? Is that why we lost our first baby?"

Harvey looks at me, a face full of concern. "No, Chelsea. Unfortunately, we won't know why you miscarried, but this isn't an issue related to drug use." He pauses for a beat before continuing, "are you using drugs now?"

"Now? No. I haven't touched them for years. I went through a rough patch and used cocaine for a few months, but I haven't even had a drop of alcohol for four years."

Harvey smiles at me and gives a faint nod. "That's good to hear. I'm glad you were able to get through that. But to answer your question again, no. You did nothing to cause this, *if* it's even an issue. Remember, we know nothing for certain. I'm just telling you this so you understand why more tests are needed. I'm not telling you to make you panic."

"Dr. Steel, Panic is my soundtrack."

He chuckles, but I'm serious. In more ways than one.

"Try to keep your stress level down as much as possible, and when you come back Friday, we'll have some answers."

I issue a silent nod, but Dola steps in to speak when I can't. "Thank you, Harvey. We'll see you on Friday."

"See the receptionist on your way out and she'll get you the appointment details. Until then, Chelsea, get plenty of rest and eat well. Those are the best things you can do right now."

I leave Dr. Steel's office, determined to follow his advice the best I can. There is absolutely nothing I wouldn't do for my babies. Resting and eating are hardly sacrifices.

Change of Heart

12

A smiling Liam with a loose tie draped around his neck, framing his handsome features, walks into our bedroom as I'm swinging my legs over the edge of the bed. "Breakfast, for my queen." He's carrying a tray of whatever he's prepared for me today. He's been taking my rest seriously and preparing breakfast before he leaves for work.

"I was on my way out to the kitchen, but thank you. I have to get up, anyway."

Those words aren't lost on him. He is as painfully aware as I am that today is the day I go for my advanced fetal imaging scan.

Thankfully, his mom could relay what the doctor said on Tuesday, because if I had to do it, I would have infused my panic level into the retelling and made Liam panic too. He's been as level-headed as ever the past two days though, taking whatever practical steps he can to make sure the babies and me are looked after.

He's already a phenomenal father. Then there's me. The can't-do-a-dang-thing-right mother. Chelsea, whatever-my-last-name-is—Wells, Haynes, Davis—doesn't make a difference. The only thing I don't fail at is failing. When it comes to failure, I'm always a success. I'm worried that will follow me into my new role as a mother.

I can't be responsible for three babies. I've never been around babies in my life. What ever made me think I'd be able to handle one—let alone three?

"Are you worried about today?"

That's a ridiculous question. I'm worried about everything. All. The. Time. "Of course, I'm worried. I've tried to be logical and remember what your mom and Dr. Steel said, but you know my worry doesn't respond well to reason."

Liam steps forward, placing the plate of fresh fruit and a bagel on the bedside table before pulling my head toward his chest. He cradles me, stroking my hair, trying to ease the mental storm raging inside me. "Whatever the results say, we'll handle it together. You and me, Babe."

"It's not us I'm worried about." I choke back my threatening tears. "I'm afraid our baby is going to have either a short life, or a miserable one, and neither option is something I can wrap my head around."

Liam heaves a deep sigh at the same time he releases me so he can lean back and meet my eyes. "Our babies are going to have the best life we can give them, and that's all we can focus on. Anything that's out of our hands, we just have to face it. But one thing I know for sure is that our babies will never feel unloved."

His intentions are good, I know that. My complicated mind can only focus on two things. First, that I spent most of my life feeling unloved, and can only hope I'll never leave any of our kids knowing that pain. Second, regardless of Liam's confidence we'll handle things, I can't just 'go with the flow' when it comes to the quality of life our children will have.

In order to placate my husband, I reply, "I know. I'll call you as soon as our appointment is finished."

Liam's face drops, and I know how hard it is for him to not be with me today. His work is pushing him to finish an extensive project, and we want to bank his time off for once the babies are born. His mother has, once again, offered to accompany me, and I'm relieved to have both her expertise and love for what lies ahead today.

With a gentle kiss, Liam tells me everything he wants to say before straightening his tie, grabbing his suit jacket, and heading out the door for work. My stomach churns at the thought of not having him with me, but I know this is for the best. Logical thought is just not my strong suit.

I munch on the food Liam brought me before I get up to shower. Eating before I get out of bed has helped to curb my nausea, but that has eased in my second trimester. Mercifully. Standing in front of the mirror, I examine my burgeoning belly. I'm curious how much bigger it's going to get. I've reached the halfway point of the expected term for triplets, but I anticipate my stomach will double its current circumference by the thirty-two-week mark.

Just as I pull my shirt over my head, our doorbell rings and I waddle-jog to answer. On the other side of our door stands the woman who raised the man I love; the grandmother who makes my future children incredibly lucky.

"Hi, Love. Are you ready?" Dola leans in, giving me a peck on the cheek and a gentle hug, which is what I've come to expect each time I see her.

"I guess so. I am eager to get this over with, but at the same time, ignorance is bliss."

She gives me an understanding smile before telling me what I need to know. "Remember what Harvey said. The imaging equipment is not perfect, and there could be nothing wrong at all. In my experience, that's often the case. This is just a precaution."

I swallow the anxiety-induced lump in my throat, nod, closing the door behind me and walk to Dola's black Range Rover, ready to go see my babies again.

As we enter the receptionist's office of the Fetal Medicine Unit at *Mount Sinai*, ready to check in for my scan, Dola keeps a tight hold on my hand. I wonder if women who have that mothering instinct can ever turn it off, because I'm not inclined to run into traffic in my mid-twenties, so I don't think she's holding my hand for safety reasons. I *could* be a flight risk if my nerves get the better of me, but I wouldn't make it any further than the nearest bathroom. If Zara were here, she'd be holding my hand too, but I didn't tell her about my appointment today, not wanting to add to her stress level.

When I'm called into the room, I have my scan performed, and the sonographer has an incredible poker face which gives nothing away. I lie back, trying my best to relax and wait for Dr. Steel to deliver the results. My suppositions and anticipation do nothing to help the situation.

An hour later, we're seated in the same room we were in a few days earlier, awaiting news on Baby B's prognosis. Dola reaches a hand up to calm my bouncing leg. "Take a breath, Love. Everything will work out."

There's a swift knock at the door before it flies open, and Dr. Steel greets us both with a wide grin. His facial expression lowers my stress level by fifty per cent before he speaks a single word. "I have good news."

"Harvey, we love good news," Dola replies.

"I thought you might. Everything looks to be perfectly fine. All three babies look to be right on track, and Baby B's liver is within normal range."

Dola and I both breathe a sigh of relief, but mine signals the start of tears streaming down my cheeks. I'm quickly the recipient of a warm embrace, and my only focus now is telling Liam. I know he's tried to seem unaffected by the potential for health issues, but he loves our babies, and this will help put his mind at ease.

Harvey spends time giving me some insight into what the next several weeks will entail. I will have a lot of appointments, and the babies will be closely monitored, but he assures me this is the standard with multiples to make sure they are growing properly. His positive demeanour gives me a little boost of confidence that our children will be okay. He also told me they determined the sex of all three babies and asked if I wanted to know. Liam and I had discussed whether we wanted to find out, but I didn't think it was an option so early. We never decided either way. I relay my uncertainty to Harvey, but he solves the problem by presenting me with a sealed envelope and informs me the results are inside.

Dola heads down to the parking garage in the elevator and instructs me to meet her at the front door, so I take the few moments to call Liam.

"Hey, Babe. How did it go?"

I choke back the tears I've just gotten a handle on. "Good. It went really good."

A few seconds pass before Liam replies, "That's a relief. What did Harvey say?"

I forget Liam knows Dr. Steel on a first name basis. I cringe at the thought of a family friend becoming familiar with my 'cave of wonders' over the course of my pregnancy. Hopefully Dola and Ian never invite us for dinner on the same night.

"He said everything looks good. Baby B is fine as far as they can tell." Despite the tears trickling down my face, I'm smiling. "He also found out the baby's sexes if we want to know. I have an envelope."

"Wow, so soon?" A pause passes while I wait for Liam to continue. "I was pretty sure I wanted to wait because I felt like meeting the babies for the first time would be even more exciting. But I think we should do it. We can do a gender reveal party if you want."

I contemplate his proposal. The surprise sounds exciting, but having three babies, preparation is a smart idea. "Okay. We can do a gender reveal with our families. But, Liam?"

"Yeah?"

"Can we keep their names to ourselves until they're born? I'd like to keep that bit of surprise."

"Of course, Babe. I have to get back to work, but let me know when Mom drops you off home, please?"

Dola rounds the corner, pulling up to the curb. Before I open the door, I assure Liam I'll let him know when we're home safely. The past few days have been marked with so much uncertainty and stress, I'm looking forward to having a night together, feeling nothing but contentment and excitement for the future.

Brain Freeze

13

Eight days ago I received the envelope indicating who are cooped up in my womb waiting to make their entrance into our lives. Eight nights I sat awake running through different scenarios based on what that envelope contains. It doesn't matter what the ratio is—I'm just happy they are healthy. Still, that doesn't lessen the excitement I'm feeling for our gender reveal shower today.

Once I returned home from my appointment, I called Zara to give her an update. She was upset I hadn't confided in her about the potential health problems, but she understood my motivations and thanked me for considering her feelings. She did, however, insist I not keep anything from her in the future regarding her grandbabies. She wants to be a part of the entire process; the ups and downs.

Zara convinced me to allow her to host our gender reveal shower as retribution for being left out of the baby's health scare. I'm not sure how she justified that was a fair trade, but I learned long ago not to argue with her once she's decided something.

Jasmine, Zach's younger sister, brought me a maternity dress for the occasion. If not for her I would have worn leggings and a sweater, but even those are getting tight. I put on the white maxi-dress with a blue and pink flowered belt. It's cute, but more importantly, it's comfortable.

As I'm pulling my hair back into a loose side braid, Liam enters the room. "Wow. You look beautiful."

"Liam. I look like an orangutan meme. How do other people make pregnant bellies look cute?"

He chuckles at me but steps forward, placing his left hand on my belly and his right arm around my back to pull me close. "You look stunning. Every time I look at you, you take my breath away. Seeing your body change to grow our children, there's nothing more beautiful than that. I love you so much, Babe. I love our babies, and I love the life we have together. Never, for one second, doubt how beautiful you are. To me, you're perfection."

Gulp. "Did you eat cheesy puffs or something, because your cheese-factor is even higher than normal." I giggle, trying to reduce the seriousness of Liam's declaration.

"Hey! I thought you liked my cheese. But I'm just being honest."

"I know you are, and I appreciate that. I just don't feel attractive at all. To be fair, I never felt attractive before I developed stretch marks and swollen ankles." I pause for a second before asking a question that's been on my mind for a few days. "Why did you stop calling me Big Red? You call me Babe now, which is fine, but I've been Big Red for years. Why?"

Liam glances around the room before his eyes settle on his fidgeting hands. "I know you're feeling a little... um... large. I didn't think being called *Big* Red would help. So I figured I'd call you Babe, because I think you are." Liam scoops me up—a remarkable feat, considering my robust middle—and carries me to the bed, gently placing me down. "Do I need to show you how much of a babe you are?"

I squeal and squirm, laughing at his antics, grateful he always stops to consider my feelings. "Liam, stop. It took me forever to get my hair presentable." Using him as a support, I pull myself to sit at the edge of the bed. "Besides, we have to leave in a minute, and Zara won't be pleased if we're late."

"I can't have my mother-in-law upset with me." He rolls his eyes and chuckles. Zara has never been upset with Liam for anything. Ever.

"Just so you know, I'm not sexy or cute, but I'm still. Big. Red."

To say my family went all out would be a gross understatement. We pull up to the huge white-stucco house and park in front of the garage. I'm giggling at the thought of Zach being instructed to hang decorations outside, knowing he'd do anything Zara asked of him, but probably wasn't thrilled about it. He could teach a master class in the "happy wife, happy life" philosophy. I appreciate them and their relationship because growing up the way I did, their example taught me how a marriage should be.

When the door flies open, I'm still standing ten feet away, gaping at the immaculate décor. When I catch Zara's eye, I wave my hand around and ask, "how did you do all of this so fast?"

"Um. Express shipping."

Bond is the first to greet us as we walk in the door, so I give him a scratch behind his ears. Isla and Zach are close behind, both wearing pink and blue outfits. Guaranteed, that's another thing Zach conceded on to please Zara. I notice Isla's shirt says, "World's Best ~~Sister~~ Aunt," and laugh at how creative they've gotten. Fred and Alanna Levy are also here, so I make my way over to greet the only grandparents I've ever known. Alanna cries as soon as I walk toward her, stopping me in my tracks, unsure of what's upset her.

"You look so beautiful," she says, and I realize they are happy tears. I don't recall seeing her cry once in the past decade, so the sight throws me. "Can I hug you?"

I appreciate that she's still respectful of my boundaries, but I've grown a lot since I was the young girl afraid of affection. "Of course." I welcome her into a brief hug before she sniffles and pulls away.

"I can't believe I'm going to be a great grandma. My goodness, life goes too fast. It feels like just yesterday I was changing Zara's poo—"

"Thanks mom! Chelsea doesn't want to hear about my dirty diapers. She'll have enough of those in her future," Zara adds as she speed-walks past carrying a massive black balloon.

I socialize with everyone on our short guest list, but it doesn't take long before I am exhausted, so I take a seat on the sofa and struggle to put my feet up on the coffee table. My ankles aren't very swollen, but enough I want to keep my feet up as much as possible.

Dola comes to take a seat in an armchair across from me as Isla parks herself beside me on the couch. Without prompting, she grabs hold of my feet, pulls them onto her lap, and begins giving me a foot massage while making casual conversation. I don't know how she knew my feet were aching, but the gesture means enough I'd consider naming a kid after her.

"So, what have you been up to now that you're done school?" I ask.

She adjusts herself in her seat and avoids eye contact. "Not a whole lot. Just working on writing and college admissions."

"Oh. Where are you applying?" I don't want to say it out loud, but the thought of her moving away for school terrifies me. Not for her sake; she's tough as nails. Selfishly, I'd miss her too much.

"I'm applying to Yorkville, University of Toronto, Sheridan, and Humber, which are all in the Toronto area. Two universities and two colleges. Jasmine says I could live with her and Rafael, but I'm trying to look into other options that are online."

Relief sweeps through me for a second. She's been homeschooled most of her life and done well with self-directed learning. I know she struggles with social anxiety and would likely have a hard time on a college campus, but even knowing that, I feel like she's selling herself short by opting for online classes. "Why are you looking online? Aren't the in-person classes much more reputable?"

She looks down at my feet again, still stroking them. "I don't want to be far away, Chels. From you. From the babies. I want to be here to help you."

I freeze for a moment, unsure of what to say. Dola chimes in, having been a silent party to our conversation. "You're a dear, Isla. I admire your loyalty to Chelsea, but I know she'd want you to make the best decision for yourself. She'll have us around to help with the babies, and Toronto isn't too far."

I smile at my mother-in-law, appreciating her insightfulness. "Exactly. My babies aren't your responsibility, and while I very much want you to be a part of their lives, I don't want you giving up yours in exchange. It doesn't have to be one or the other."

"That's what Mom said." She chuckles. "I don't feel like I'm giving anything up, though. You know I wouldn't enjoy typical college life, and I like directing my learning rather than being told what to learn, when. If I have a choice, I want to do school online. I just want to be close to you guys, too. To me, it's the best of both worlds."

I attempt to fold myself over and get closer to her so I can give her a hug, but my belly interferes, and my effort is met with an involuntary grunt. Isla laughs at my performance and leans in to give me a hug instead.

"You are the best sister-slash-aunt, you know? I love you, Troublemaker."

"I love you, too."

Interrupting our emotional moment, Zara chimes in, "Okay, we're going to find out the sex of the babies, but we wanted to celebrate each one individually rather than doing them all at once. So, Chels, Liam, are you ready to find out if Baby A is a boy or a girl?"

I look at Liam and see him smiling so wide, his face is nearly split in half. He gives me a nod and reaches his hand out to take mine. He hoists me off of the couch and we walk over to the black balloon I saw Zara carrying earlier.

Liam and I stand on either side of the balloon, staring out at the seven most important people in our lives—eight, including Bond—who are looking back at us through cell phone cameras, ready to capture the moment.

Liam reaches behind the balloon strings to take my hand. "Are you ready, Momma?"

I return his wide smile. "I'm ready, Daddy."

He waggles his eyebrows at me, and I can't help but laugh. "One, two, three." *Pop!*

A mass of baby blue balloons fall to the floor and everyone shouts, "it's a boy!"

I sidestep through the balloon mess to pull Liam in for a hug. I can't help but cry happy tears and realize how nonsensical that is, because I would have been equally as happy if the balloons were pink. There's just something about knowing who exists inside me that has my emotions reaching a boiling point.

Fred is the first to ask, "Do you have any names picked out?"

I eye Liam, who replies, "No, not yet. We'll have to work on that."

"I've always been partial to the name Frederick, myself." Everyone laughs, and we spend the next hour socializing; me mostly from my perch on the sofa.

Zara interrupts the chatter, "it's time for baby B's moment, then we'll eat dinner."

This time she has a box set up where the balloon had been previously. Liam and I take our positions, and once everyone has their cameras poised and ready, he rips off the tape. A rush of blue balloons fly to the ceiling.

"Another boy!" everyone shouts, followed by giggles.

I'm staring off into space, imagining our two baby boys. I'm so curious what they'll look like. If they'll have my ginger hair, or Liam's skin tone. Will they have similar personalities, or be complete opposites of each other? I'm so excited to get to know them, and grateful they'll have wonderful men in their lives to learn from.

Liam pulls me into his arms and kisses me. "You're really outnumbered now, Babe."

"I'm so happy." I can't say anything else because I'm sobbing like a stereotypical, emotional pregnant woman.

"Me too."

After we eat dinner, Zara presents an elaborately decorated cake made by her friend Desirea of *Desirea's Sweets*—Zara's go-to bakery. I'm absolutely stuffed, but nothing is going to stop me from learning who else is joining our family.

As Liam and I stand behind the cake at the end of the large dining table, surrounded by our loved ones, I know whatever the colour is inside this cake won't matter. Regardless, this baby will be loved and cherished, just as the two boys will be.

Liam and I each place a hand on the long cake knife that we used to slice our wedding cake over two years ago, and I recognize how far we've come from the two anti-social teens listening to *Panic! At The Disco* in my bedroom doing English homework.

The knife sinks into the cake, and we remove it to cut a slice. I take a deep breath as we lift it and see a blue strip of icing in the middle.

"Three boys!" Everyone cheers.

"Our boys." Liam leans me back and kisses me in front of everyone.

In the Same Vein

14

Twenty-six weeks pregnant with triplets is not comfortable. Nor attractive. The first time I felt one of the boys' kicks, I was beyond excited. The first time a kick was strong enough for Liam to feel one, he was overjoyed. Now, they're just in there like the Karate Kids, with an affinity for tapdancing on my bladder. I can barely sleep. Getting out of a chair takes effort rivaling an Olympic decathlon, and I'm seriously considering painting over our bathroom mirror.

I'm living in Liam's clothes now. Once he complained about me stretching out his t-shirts. Once. Now he knows better.

Safe to say, I'm freaking miserable. If I'm not asleep, I'm tired; no, I'm exhausted. If I'm not keeping my mind occupied with something, I'm sitting around doubting my mothering abilities, and fearing for the future my children will face. It's probably uncommon for anyone to go into parenthood with great confidence, but I have zero.

Not to mention, after a long discussion with Liam, we agreed it was best I take a leave of absence from work and prioritize the babies' safety, so I've been bored out of my mind. If I'm being totally honest though, I was too tired to be efficient at work.

There have been no major issues with my pregnancy since our scare at sixteen weeks, but that doesn't mean it's been easy. The travel back and forth for appointments is exhausting, and while I'm grateful Dola has been available to take me, I am feeling a little resentful of Liam's job because he hasn't been able to be present. At times, it's as if I'm going through this process alone, and it's wearing on me, worried that raising our kids will be the same. His work obligations won't change just because our children vacate my body. How is Liam going to cope with work and home demands? He might be a great man, but he's not Superman.

I'm lying on the sofa with the TV on, but not watching it. Reading was a lost cause because I couldn't focus. I just keep spiralling down the "I know I'm going to be a terrible mother" train of thought.

Ding Dong.

No one called to say they were coming, so the doorbell catches me by surprise. I'm tempted to ignore it in hopes whoever it is will go away, but I know no one would show up here without good reason.

I waddle to the door to find the woman who was the first person to love me. The first person whom I loved in return.

"Hi, Sweetheart. Sorry to just drop by, but I was driving home and had this overwhelming feeling to stop in." She peeks her head past me through the door. "Are you busy?"

I look down at myself—braless, wearing Liam's stretched t-shirt with a grease stain on my left boob, and track pants. Nailing this hot-mess-mom business. "No, I'm not busy. Just being a lazy blob. Same as yesterday."

Zara's eyes drop, scanning my ever-growing midsection. "Do you want to go for a little walk? The weather is beautiful. Some fresh air might feel good."

I immediately want to dismiss her proposal but decide a little outside time might help. I've been staring at the same four walls for days, and aside from appointments haven't been out of the house much for weeks.

"Okay. I doubt I'll make it further than the end of the driveway, but a short walk might be nice. Just let me change." I gesture with my head for her to come inside while I go put on something more presentable.

When I return from my bedroom, sweaty from the effort of putting a different pair of pants on, I find Zara doing my dishes. As pathetic as it is, even bending to put dishes in the dishwasher is a challenge, and my belly interferes too much to reach the sink to wash things by hand. So, that's another task that has been added to Liam's growing list of responsibilities.

"You don't have to do that."

"Chels. I know I don't *have* to do it. I want to do it. It looks like you could use a little help. Why haven't you called?"

Why haven't I? Because I've been nothing but a burden for my entire life and asking for assistance is not something I do easily. I've learned the hard way that resisting help is dangerous mindset to get into, but my inability to rely on others has been a harder habit to break than my cocaine addiction.

"You know I don't like to bother anyone. Liam and I are managing."

"You are not a bother. You're forgetting that we love you and these babies. I know Dola has been helping get you to appointments, so the least I can do is some housework." She sets down the sponge and walks around the island. "I'm going to come on Mondays and Thursdays. Those are my slow days, and I could use some time out of the house." Zara works out of their home as a counsellor, so she is familiar with the feeling of seeing your own four walls too much.

"I don't want you spending your time off cleaning our house. Liam said we could hire a cleaning service to come a few times a week until after the babies are born, but we've just been putting off any unnecessary expenses."

Zara appears to have a 'lightbulb' moment. "Well, consider me your cleaning service. Free of charge. If I come and you don't need anything done, we can do something else. Meal prep, back massage. Whatever you need. Count on me."

I chuckle at her determination. Zara, despite her own struggles with anxiety and depression, is a force to be reckoned with. Nothing short of a herd of wild horses would stop her from accomplishing something she sets her mind to, so I don't argue.

"Okay. Let's see if I can make it to the mailbox and back." I laugh at the truth in that statement, because 400 metres round trip shouldn't be a challenge, but when your body is sustaining a third of a baseball team, walking to the toilet is an accomplishment.

We're mere feet from the front door when Zara gets to the serious stuff. "So, how are you feeling otherwise? I know physically you must be uncomfortable..." She watches me waddle as the side of her mouth turns up, and I can only imagine how amusing it looks to everyone else. "But I want to know how you're doing emotionally. Mentally."

Forever in counsellor mode. I can't bring myself to look at her because I'm not prepared to be honest right now. "I'm fine. It's normal for new parents to have fears and worries."

"Well, yes and no. It's normal to have some fears and worries, yes, but there are healthy and unhealthy levels of each. What do you worry about specifically?"

I didn't know this was going to turn into an exercise and therapy session, but I can't deny that Zara has always had my best interests at heart, even when I didn't see it.

"I guess the biggest thing is the fear that I'll fail as a mom. One child is hard enough, but three? Just trying to figure out how to balance my time between them equally, treating them fairly, and making sure they all feel loved."

A few steps later, Zara responds, "I think the important distinction there, Chels, is that fair doesn't always mean equal. Each child, even with triplets, will come with their own personalities and needs. What one child needs won't be the same as what the others need. So, focus on being fair, not equal."

"I suppose. But I want them all to know they're loved. You know that's something I struggled with, and I never want them to feel that way."

She stops walking and scrutinizes my face. "The fact you've even thought about that tells me they'll always know they're loved. People who fail to show their children love—people like your biological father—they don't consider how their child feels. You are not your father."

I nod, choking down the lump in my throat.

"When Zach and I adopted you and Isla, I was terrified. I had no idea what I was doing, and I had the same fears. I worried you both wouldn't feel loved, or I would screw you up. Quinn went through the same feelings when Leo was born. Parenting doesn't come with a manual."

This is news to me. She never let on that she had any of those fears. "You have been a great mom. Right from the start, and even during the times when I couldn't see it at the moment. Looking back, you were always exactly what we needed."

Zara's lips curl into a smile. "Thank you for saying that. My point is, I was told very early on, 'if you spend your life trying to be perfect, you're just going to miss out on all the good.' The best thing you can do is to keep loving them. Love them through the hard times and struggles. Love them when you don't feel worthy of it yourself. Love is the goal, and it's the one thing that will matter in the long run."

Just keep loving them. I think I can do that.

Under My Skin

15

iam and I are standing in what will be our babies' nursery. It took me weeks to decide on a theme because I didn't want to go "all out" just to have to redecorate once they turn one and their needs change. I didn't realize babies came with so much stuff, so I've been standing in the middle of the room, spinning in circles, unsure where to put everything.

"I feel like I'm stuffocating."

He glances at me with a raised eyebrow and a smirk. "You mean suffocating?"

"No. Stuffocating. We have so much stuff, I can't breathe. This looks like an episode of hoarders and I'm afraid if we put a baby in here, we won't even be able to find him later."

Liam chuckles. "That's a new one. I know it's a lot, but we have time to get it all sorted. Don't worry. We'll get it ready for them and won't lose any babies. We still have the extra room upstairs, so I can take anything we won't use until they're older up there."

I feel better after that suggestion, but we are running out of time. At thirty-two weeks pregnant, it's possible for the babies to come any time now.

Liam spends the next several hours taking one thing after another upstairs to our unused bedroom. When we moved into this house, we assumed it would be our forever home and we'd have more space than we'd ever know what to do with. Turns out, three babies change that in a hurry.

I'm not sure why, but Liam has been distant the past few days, and my hormonal self can't handle it a minute longer. Before he makes his way back upstairs with the next jumparoo, I ask, "why do I feel like you're avoiding me today? Have I done something wrong?"

He sets down the baby gear and runs his hands through his overgrown curly hair. "I was trying to find the right time to tell you, but I don't think there is a good time."

The absence of his nickname for me and seriousness in his voice has me panicking before he speaks another word. "Are you divorcing me?"

"What? No. Of course not, Chels. You're my whole world." He sighs and sits on the charcoal-grey pull-out sofa we placed under the window in case either of us needs to crash in the babies' room. He folds himself over with his elbows on his knees, head in his hands. "I have to go away for work next week."

That's not divorce-level bad, but it's pretty darn close. "What do you mean 'away?' I could go into labour at any time. Did you tell your boss that? Can't someone else go?"

"Babe, I tried. I promise, I made no less than fifty alternative suggestions, but they weren't happy with any of them. I have to go to Chicago Monday morning, and I'll be back Friday evening."

Unsure what to say in response to that, I opt for nothing. I waddle out of our babies' room with tears in my eyes. Liam's job is our livelihood, so some concessions have to be made.

However, I thought that's what the missed appointments were over the past five months. It never occurred to me he'd miss the birth of our children; that I'd have to go through the hardest part alone.

I walk through our bedroom, into our ensuite, and lock the door behind me. It wasn't my intention to have a shower, but right now, it's the best place to have a good cry.

I haven't expressed to Liam how scared I am to have these babies. Not raising them and being a decent mother—we've talked about that. I mean the actual birthing process. Having a c-section to remove three babies out of me is terrifying. Sure, the medical staff are experienced, but things still go wrong. What if something happens to me and he's not there?

The hot water streams down on me for twenty minutes before I sit on the shower bench, letting the water wash away my stress and worries. It's doing a terrible job.

My first attempt to stand fails. My stomach is so heavy and awkward, I can't get enough momentum to get up from my slippery seat. My second attempt fails. Five minutes later, all subsequent attempts have failed. I resign myself to the fact I need help, and since I can't reach my phone to check Amazon for pregnant-lady cranes, I have only one choice.

"Liam?"

He doesn't even reply. The doorknob rattles for a split second before Liam comes bursting through the door like the Kool-Aid man. "Are you okay? What's wrong?"

I stare at him, mouth wide open. "You could have asked that from the other side of the door before you added another item to your to-do list."

"Uh. Yeah. Sorry. I panicked."

"I see that." Laughing is not an option right now because I'm angry with him, so I paste my scowl back on my face. "I'm stuck. I can't get up."

He looks relieved, but this is not the best-case scenario. Especially with him leaving in two days. "Is that why you've been in here for so long?"

"No, Liam. I was in here crying because I'm about to give birth to three babies, and my husband has decided a work trip is more important." The fury gives me the strength I need, and I use my upper body to push off the wall and stand. "Good thing I don't need your help."

"Babe. I don't want this. It wasn't my decision."

"Last I checked, you were a grown man, Liam. You can make your own decisions."

"And then what, Chels? Lose my job? Have no way to keep a roof over our heads, or feed our babies? I'm trying here. I really am. Not every decision is simple to make, but I'm doing what I feel like I have to do so you guys are taken care of. I'm not choosing my job over you or our babies." He tosses me a towel and turns to walk out of the room.

I realize I was too hard on him, and instinctively sit back down on the shower bench. Well, this is awkward. "Liam?"

His face peeks around the door frame. "Yeah?"

"Um. I'm sorry. I'm just scared. I know you're in a tough spot, and I'm sorry for not considering your perspective."

"I'm sorry too." When he walks closer and I can see him clearly through the bathroom fog, he has tears in his eyes. For a man who rarely cries, having babies sure has made him a softie. "I don't want to miss our babies being born, and I don't want to not be there for you. There's just no other choice if I want to keep my job."

"We'd find another way. There are lots of companies who would be happy to have you."

"Not here. Maybe in Toronto, sure. I'd have options. But if we want to stay here, close to our families, I can't afford to burn my bridges at this company. They know they have me in a tight spot, and they don't care."

It infuriates me to think this multi-million-dollar company is essentially holding Liam's ability to support his family hostage, but I know he's right. In our area, the job market isn't saturated with loads of opportunity. When he graduated, the job was ideal; it allowed us to buy our home and achieve the goals we set in place. But for them to interfere with Liam being present for the birth of our children, best believe that won't be forgotten.

After a few seconds of silence, I remember why I called him back. "Liam?"

"Yeah?"

"I'm stuck again."

He laughs, but I see the worry etched on his face. If something like this happens while he's away, what am I supposed to do? I can't very well call the fire department to come get me up.

Liam places one arm under each of mine and hoists me up like a forklift. It's mortifying. I wrap the towel around myself, and what previously had a solid eight-inch overlap now has an eight-inch gap.

Liam is studying me when I glance at him. "I'm really going to miss you," he says as he wraps his arms around me. Well, let's be honest—not all the way around; he's not Stretch Armstrong. "If anything happens, I'll be on the first flight back, okay?"

Hearing him say that makes me feel less concerned. "Okay."

Liam leans in to kiss me, which requires some maneuvering, but he makes it worth the hassle. "I love you so much. Nothing will keep me away from being by your side. I promise."

He hasn't disappointed me yet.

Lost My Nerve

16

Monday morning, Liam is up by 4:30am to get to the airport. Yesterday he made it his mission to equip every room in the house with *Alexa*, so if I can't get up and can't reach my phone, I can call for help. He might as well have gotten me a life-alert. It gives me a little more peace of mind, though.

Isla is in our guest room and offered to stay with me while Liam is gone. She often does anyway, but this time, I felt it was a necessary precaution. There's no telling when these babies will make their great escape.

"I'll keep my phone on at all times, even in meetings. So, call me any time. I'll check in as often as I can, and like I said, first hint of action, I'll be at the airport. I don't care if they fire me."

Every time Liam leaves, I worry about plane crashes, muggings, natural disasters… the list is endless. This time, though, there's only one concern on my mind. Only one 'what-if' scenario I'm focused on.

I tamp down my whirling anxieties because I know this is hard for him, too. "I'll text you throughout the day, but I won't call unless it's an emergency. You call me when you have free time. But if you get a call from me, then you'll know."

"Okay. It's going to be fine, Babe. Everything will be fine." He gives me a kiss, then pulls the blanket down and my shirt up to expose my massive, stretch-mark-covered stomach. "Be good for mommy and wait in there until Daddy gets home. Okay, boys?" He kisses my belly and two out of three boys respond by trying to kick his face, making Liam laugh. He gives me another kiss, and when he tries to stand, I cling to his shirt, afraid to let go. "I have to leave, Babe. I'm sorry, but Dad's outside."

"Do you think if you missed your flight, they'd just reschedule for next year or something?" My attempts at keeping my emotions at bay have failed. I'm ugly crying.

"I wish. I'd much rather crawl back in bed with you." With one last kiss on my cheek, he pulls away. "I'll be back before you know it. Just keep those babies cooking. I love you."

With that, he disappears out the door and I shout behind him, "I love you, too."

Ninety minutes later, Liam texts me from the airport to say he arrived safely, and he's at his gate. I barely had time to come to terms with him leaving before he was headed to the airport and the reality brings a flood of wracking sobs. I lie on my side, using multiple pillows to get comfortable, to no avail, crying into Liam's pillow so I can at least smell him. He smells like Irish Spring soap and Liam. His own unique smell. My favourite smell in the world.

I'm lost in my tears when the bed dips behind me. For a split second I think maybe it's Liam, and he's come back home, but when a skinny arm wraps around me, I realize who it is.

"Don't worry, Chels. He'll be home soon."

I hope so. But for the next two hours, I lie wrapped in my little sister's arms, spending more of my life worried about what's to come.

I wake from a nap a few hours later, and I hear clanking in the kitchen. I take a significant chunk of time to get myself out of bed, but I manage. Throwing on a pair of wouldn't-be-caught-dead-out-of-the-house-in-these sweatpants and one of Liam's shirts I spend a few moments sniffing, I waddle to the kitchen to find Isla and Zara.

"Hi, Sweetheart. I hope we didn't wake you."

"No, I cried myself into a coma. My bladder woke me up. What are you doing here?"

"It's Monday, remember? Since your housework looks done, I decided I'd prepare some freezer meals for you."

"Freezer meals?"

"I saw it on Pinterest. There are loads of recipes, and you take one day to shop and prepare everything, then as you need them, you just take them out of the freezer and throw them in the oven or crockpot. Instant dinner." Through that short monologue, Zara didn't stop moving. She's mixing, chopping, and boiling who-knows-what. Isla is standing silently beside her, chopping vegetables.

"That sounds helpful. Especially once the babies are here."

"That's the idea. You'll be so tired, but healthy meals are important, so I'm going to spend today getting you a head start. You go rest on the couch and holler if you need something."

"I can hel—"

"You most certainly will not. Go sit your behind on the sofa, Chelsea. Grandma's orders." She looks up at me, her green eyes bulging out of her head. "I still can't get used to the idea of being a grandma."

I laugh. She is a young grandma and I almost feel guilty. She'll be the youngest grandmother at the playground, that's for sure. I'm assuming it's uncommon to have three grandchildren before forty. "You're going to be a great grandma. You are a phenomenal mom."

Her smile is genuine, reaching her eyes, turning them into slits. "Thank you, Chels. That means everything to me. You guys were easy to love."

I laugh again, because I know that's not true. I made things anything but easy. "That's a funny joke. Isla has made things pretty easy. Even Bond, once he got over his habit of weaponizing poop. But I definitely didn't make anything easy."

Isla ceases her chopping to look at Zara, who doesn't bat an eye before replying. "Don't for one second think that making bad choices ever made me love you less. You can still love someone when you don't love their choices."

Her words stick with me. I believe that's true, but I don't think I've been remotely deserving of the kindness both mine and Liam's families have shown me over the years. If nothing else, it motivates me to earn the love they give me. I never want to disappoint them again.

I take my seat, perched on the sofa, and flip on the TV. I scroll through the Netflix menu several times. Attempt to watch a few new movies that sound interesting, but never make it past five minutes into any of them. Finally I settle on *Hot Fuzz*, because British comedy is the gold standard as far as I'm concerned.

When my phone buzzes a short time later, I glance down to read it.

Liam: I miss you. How are you feeling?

Chelsea: I'm fine, but missing you too. Mom is here making us food. Watching a movie now. Been instructed not to lift a finger.

Liam: Listen to your mother. I owe her big time. What are you watching?

Chelsea: Hot Fuzz

Liam: Good choice. I'm going into a meeting now, but I'll call when I'm done. I love you.

Chelsea: I love you too. Go get 'em, tiger.

It's amazing how even reading words Liam writes can make me feel closer to him. He's travelled plenty of times over the years, but not since I found out I was pregnant. I assumed this contract had been forgotten, or the deal didn't go through. Lesson learned. Don't make assumptions because you get blindsided by unexpected work trips when you're thirty-two weeks pregnant with triplets.

"How's it going in there?" I shout from our family room into the kitchen.

"Almost done our first batch of meals. Do you need anything?"

Just my husband. And a toilet. And maybe a crane.

Rough Road A-head

17

Liam has been gone for two days and he must have called at least sixty-three times. Isla has been a trooper, helping me whenever I get stuck, whether or not I'm clothed. I'm pretty sure she's never having kids now. She's traumatized for life.

I'm resting as much as possible, but even for an introverted bookworm, that gets boring, so I'm trying to make dinner for Isla and me then we're planning a movie night. A good-old-fashioned rom-com sesh featuring Jennifer Lopez because she can sympathize with my current condition.

As I'm standing in front of the stove, arms outstretched to their limit so I can tend to the pasta without burning my belly, I feel an intense tightening of my abdomen. I've been cramping since yesterday, but it never evolved into anything and wasn't too painful. This, well it's like someone put my stomach in a vise. I drop the wooden spoon and let out a loud groan.

"What's wrong?" Isla comes running to my side. "Chels, what's wrong?"

Her repeated pleas do nothing to encourage me to speak. The pain is intense, but the panic, even more so.

"Should I call an ambulance? What do I do?"

A few deep breaths, all I can say is, "call Dola."

Isla helps me get to the couch while she's on the phone with my mother-in-law and lifts my feet. I hear her saying "I don't know," repeatedly before placing the phone on the coffee table on speaker.

"Chelsea. Tell me what's happening? I'm on my way now."

I feel a wave of relief knowing she's coming. Not just because of her medical expertise, but because I know she loves these babies as much as I do, and she'll make sure we make the right decision.

"It hurts."

"Okay, Love. What hurts? Does it get worse, then relax?"

"Uh-huh." I let out another pained groan as the pain surges again.

"I'm a few minutes away. Isla, hang up and call an ambulance, okay? I think Chelsea's going into labour."

That's what I was afraid of. "Liam."

"I know, Love. I'm going to call him now. Just breathe, and I'll be right there."

Isla disconnects the call and immediately dials 911. She's still speaking to the dispatcher when Dola barges through the front door, clearly on the phone with Liam. "Okay, dear. I'll call you back when I know something." She rushes over to me, examining me briefly. "Liam is going to head to the airport now. We just need these little guys to hang on. Do you think we can do that?"

The pain has eased for a moment. "They seem to have plans of their own. It feels like they're tearing me in twooooooo..." That didn't last long.

I try to focus my breathing as I wait for the paramedics to arrive, hopeful they have some magic concoction that will make this pain stop.

Two hours later, I'm lying in a hospital bed at *Mount Sinai*. Dola insisted I be brought here and she was determined enough, no one argued. Dr. Steel came in to check on me when I arrived, and they gave me Terbutaline to slow the progression of labour.

A thorough inspection of my 'love tunnel' reveals I'm three centimetres dilated. I'm told this means I'm not quite in active labour, but they've given me a needle in my butt that's supposed to help the babies' lungs develop. Hopefully I can hold them in for twenty-four hours. I'll have to stay in the hospital until the babies are born, which could be today, or a few days from now, depending on what the monitors pick up.

Dola hasn't left my side and promises she won't. Isla went home to update Zara and Zach. They're staying put for now until we have more information about when the babies will arrive. There's no use in them coming to hang out in my hospital room when I'm meant to be resting.

When Dola's phone rings, she answers in a whisper. A second later, she passes the phone to me with a sombre expression. "It's Liam, Love."

"Liam?"

"Hi, Babe. How are you holding up?"

"I'm scared, and I wish you were here. But your mom is taking good care of us."

"I wish I was there, too. That's why I was calling." He releases a frustrated sigh. "I've spent ninety minutes trying every option, but nothing is available to get me home until tomorrow."

My heart drops. He promised. He told me he'd be here. I don't get to respond before another wave of pain takes over. I let out a wail.

"Chels? Oh, Babe. I'm so sorry. I'm going to find a way. I love you."

I hand the phone back to Dola, who relays updates to Liam before hanging up.

The tears that had been on account of the pain earlier are now attributed to my heart breaking.

Dola grabs my hand and wipes my cheeks. "He's going to find a way, Love. One thing I know about my son is that he'll make things happen when he's determined enough. And until then, I'm not going anywhere."

I close my eyes, squeezing the remaining tears to slide down my face.

"You know, I only had one child because Ian and I weren't able to conceive more. I always wanted to have a daughter. Even though I wasn't able to have one in the traditional way, I couldn't be more grateful to have you now. I know you have Zara, but I love you like you're my child, and I hope you see me as a bonus mother."

Well, she's not doing much to quell my emotional outpour. Her admission opens my floodgates until she grabs a damp cloth to dab my forehead, brushing my hair from my face, and helping to keep my body temperature comfortable.

"Thank you, Mom," I choke out. It took me years to refer to Zara as my mom because I didn't feel I deserved the love of someone befitting that moniker. It wasn't until Liam and I had been dating for a few weeks that I felt comfortable calling her mom. Imagine that. Having a twenty-one-year-old reformed drug addict calling you mom for the first time. You would have thought I handed her the moon. But now, I'm lucky enough to have two inspiring women, each with their own talents and strengths, to see me through the most challenging parts of my life. That's saying a lot given my life has been a sequence of trials and tribulations.

I'm able to get comfortable enough to catch a few hours of sleep, waking up briefly when the nurse comes in to check the beeping monitors and write down any changes.

Glancing at my phone, I have no updates from Liam and I hope that means he's on an airplane to somewhere that will lead him home. Dola is asleep in the vinyl recliner situated beside my bed and would hear nothing of going home for some proper rest. I was relieved she refused to leave.

She stirs when I set my phone back down on the table. "Anything from Liam?"

"No. Nothing."

Offering a weak smile, she gives me some more reassurance and I can only hope I'll be as confident in my sons when they're older. I rub a hand across my belly, willing my babies to sense how much I love them. They've been uncharacteristically lazy the past day or so, and if it weren't for the rhythmic beating of their heartbeats on the monitors, I'd be even more of a mess right now.

I allow the steady rhythm to lull me back to sleep.

When I'm awoken by tensing in my stomach and beeping alarms, I see the commotion of two nurses through my bleary eyes.

Dola is standing at my bedside, holding my left hand in hers, and her right hand on my shoulder. "Love. It's time. They can't wait any longer."

"What? No. Liam isn't here. What's wrong? Why can't they wait?"

She rubs my shoulder as her soft eyes express one of my worst fears. "One of the babies' heart rate keeps dropping, and they need to get him out. He could be in distress."

Distress? No. The only thing I want more than Liam being present is for our babies to be healthy and safe, so I nod my understanding. I may not have Liam, but I have the rest of my family and an expert medical team.

The medical staff are coming and going, writing things down, checking my IV, prepping me for a spinal, and giving me the rundown about what will happen. I don't know if anyone ever feels prepared for this moment, but ready or not, here they come.

They give me the go ahead and start wheeling my bed out of the room. They usher Dola off to scrub in and change her clothes. She's in her element, but I can't help but wish it were Liam in her place.

As I enter the bright operating room, my heart rate is accelerating, and I'm trying to suppress the impending panic vomit. When the anesthesiologist comes to insert the spinal, I'm asked to drape my legs from the side of the bed, fold over as much as I can, and stay still. I've been terrified of having an epidural or spinal since before we started talking about getting pregnant and I feel an overwhelming sense of panic. "Please, can my mother-in-law come in?"

The anesthesiologist replies, "unfortunately, no. This is a sterile procedure."

My eyes, which seem to have a never-ending supply of tears, are pouring again, but my panic turns me into a possessed psychopath. "Then hose her down and put her in a HAZMAT suit!"

The doctor pauses for a moment and gestures toward a nurse who walks closer to me, probably deciding if she gets enough danger pay to approach. When she stands in front of me, I cling to her like a baby opossum latches on its mother.

After two attempts, on account of me not being able to stay still, the spinal is inserted, and my lower half is well on its way to being numbed.

I'm equipped with an oxygen mask to help keep my breathing in check, and a curtain to prevent me from seeing my guts being emptied. I'm grateful for both. The doctor is speaking to me, asking if I have questions, but I'm so focused on keeping calm, there's nothing else I want to know. I close my eyes and vow to keep them closed until I hear my babies cry.

A warm hand touches the bare skin on my arm, and when I glance up, I see the watery eyes of my husband.

"Hi, Babe. I told you I'd make it."

I Can't Stomach it

18

My husband made a nine-hour drive in seven hours, twenty-two minutes in a rental car he negotiated away from an elderly couple who couldn't stop bickering. Liam's offer of a hefty wad of cash settled their disputes. He promised he'd be here, and he is. As soon as I felt his touch, my fears surrounding childbirth were halved. Not because he has any medical expertise, but because I don't have to hide my fears from him and he helps me carry the weight of them.

The room is crowded with various medical staff and equipment. There are three NICU teams on standby to tend to each baby as they're born. Knowing that is both concerning and comforting. I'm just shy of thirty-three weeks, which is normal for triplets but still seven weeks premature. I hope all three boys are born with some of the tenacity I've had over the course of my life, but without the turmoil.

When the doctor indicates he's ready to begin, I look at Liam, who bends down to place his forehead against mine. "You've got this. Let's meet our boys."

"Let's meet our boys," I reply.

Baby A is born at 4:33am, weighing three pounds eleven ounces. He has a full head of medium brown hair, and an alarming amount of body hair. The nurse who shows him to us assures me that is normal. I've never seen a hairy baby before, but he's beautiful. Liam gushes over his little nose and tiny fingers, but the first NICU team ushers him off quickly as he needs some assistance breathing.

We don't have the chance to panic too much before Baby B arrives at 4:37am, weighing four pounds, two ounces, looking just like his older brother. I suppose a lifetime as the middle child isn't so bad when you're only four minutes younger. I'm able to reach out and touch his little toes before he's swept away by the second NICU team.

Baby C comes into the world at 4:49am after he gave the doctors a scare, but is the first of the three to let out a muffled cry. The sound is the most beautiful thing I've ever heard. At three pounds, four ounces, he's the smallest, but I'm told their weights are average for their gestational age.

"Look, Babe. He has your hair!"

When I examine the newest member of our family, I notice he has a full head of straight, coppery hair—granted, he is covered in womb goo. His features look much like his big brothers', but he's got his own unique look. My baby boy.

Liam and I are given some time alone in my recovery room, with frequent interruptions from nurses, and one from the doctor who performed my cesarean. As far as they're concerned, things went well, and despite warnings of some pain while I recover, they have no major worries. That's a relief, but my focus is on my babies. I want to see them more than anything. The last nurse said I can see them shortly, and I'm counting the minutes.

We settle on our babies' names, content knowing we'll be shouting them hundreds of times over the next few decades.

When I'm given the thumbs up to see the babies, I would jump with joy if I wasn't worried about my innards landing on the polished concrete floor. That would put a damper on the day.

I take a seat in an elaborate semi-reclined wheelchair, and Liam is instructed to have me back in bed within the hour. I have sixty minutes to see my babies and I don't want to waste a single one.

We round the corner into the hallway en route to the NICU and find our families waiting for an update. Their expressions are a mix of excitement and concern. As soon as they see us, each one of them drops their shoulders a couple of inches. How they got here before 7am is a wonder.

"They're here," Liam declares, which is met by cheers and hugs. "They're all in the NICU, so you can see them, but they only allow two people at a time. I think their Momma should see them first." Everyone nods in agreement, which I wouldn't expect otherwise.

Before we can get any further, Zach asks, "what did you name them?"

I smile and glance at Liam. He nods for me to share the names we've chosen. "Well, when we took our honeymoon to New York, we spent a lot of time exploring different neighbourhoods. First, we went to Chelsea, because Liam wanted to take pictures of me with everything that had my name." Everyone chuckles because that's a very cheesy Liam thing to do. "So we gave the babies all New York City names. Baby A is Hudson, like Hudson Yards. Hudson Zachary."

I look at Zach and his eyes widen with surprise. "Really?"

"Really. You were the first man I ever trusted. The first one I loved. Giving our son your name is the least I can do to repay you for everything." He nods but doesn't speak. He's clearly surprised. "Baby B is Lincoln, like Lincoln Square. Lincoln Frederick."

Zara gasps. "Oh, Dad will be so happy."

"I hope so. He welcomed me into the family without hesitation, and I hope our son grows up to be as wonderful as my grandpa." I turn to look at Liam's father. "Baby C, our little ginger, is Lenox. From Lenox Hill. Lenox Ian Davis."

Ian looks at his son, then at me. "After me?"

Liam and I both laugh.

"Yes, Dad. Of course, after you. You taught me everything about being a man and a father. I love you, old man."

"I love you too, son. I love you both." Everyone exchanges hugs, but I'm getting impatient, wanting to see my babies.

Before we can get away, Zach asks, "so, if you ever get a dog, are you going to name him Yonkers?" He laughs at his own joke, and I roll my eyes at his attempted humour.

Zara chimes in, "no. They'd name it Sugar. She told me their favourite neighbourhood was Sugar Hill."

Her comment startles me. I've been so distracted by the events of the day, it's the first time I haven't thought about Sugar. Our one baby who should have been here, but we were given three instead. I never would have chosen to lose our first baby, but if Sugar was here, Lincoln, Hudson, and Lenox wouldn't be. As hard as the journey was, I have to look at the bright side.

Liam gives me a squeeze on my shoulder, and I assume he's having the same thoughts as me. He informs everyone we're going to see our babies, and wheels me down the hallway.

When we round the corner into the NICU, there seems to be a lot of commotion. I sympathize with the family whose baby warrants such a kerfuffle, because in neonatal intensive care, I would imagine it's not a good sign. When we enter the ward our babies are in, Liam stops in his tracks and turns white as a sheet of paper. It only takes me a split second to realize why.

Lenox has a team of doctors and nurses surrounding him, with one issuing determined instructions to everyone else. It's a good thing I'm in a wheelchair, or I might have collapsed to the floor.

"What's happening? What's wrong with our baby?"

You take My Breath Away

19

Pneumothorax. I'd never heard that word before, and I never want to again. Lenox's right lung collapsed, and he couldn't breathe. He's being equipped for transport to neighbouring *SickKids Hospital* where he will be put on a different ventilator and given a few days to recover. He has a tube through his tiny chest, which was required to drain the air from his chest cavity.

I can't let go of his little hand. He was fighting for his life and I didn't even know. Aren't mothers supposed to have a sixth sense about these things? Shouldn't I have been able to tell something was wrong? He hasn't been out of my body for more than a few hours, and I've already failed him.

"We're going to transfer him now. They have a bed available, and they're going to take good care of him." A member of the *SickKids* Transport Team speaks to me, but I barely acknowledge her words. I couldn't describe her, because I can't take my eyes off of Lenox.

I've been told I can't go with him because I am still a patient, but Liam can. Before he goes, he leans down to kiss my forehead. "He's going to be fine. I know you're scared for him, but he is going to the best children's hospital in the world. They don't get that title for nothing."

I hold back my tears because I don't want to make leaving me harder for Liam. He follows our baby out of the room in a travelling incubator, surrounded by two transport team members.

I ask to be positioned in between Lincoln and Hudson's cots, and I sit there taking in their features. They have near identical noses, and the same dark hair, but Lincoln has fuller lips, like his dad. Hudson has more body hair—I'm really hoping they're serious when they say that's normal and it will fall out. He's like a little teddy bear. I knew time in the NICU was likely, and I wanted to share my love for books, so I take out a few of the books I packed and begin reading.

Do Not Wish For A Pet Ostrich is a hit with Lincoln, and I have a feeling that means he's going to be cheeky. As I read, he opened his eyes, and while I know he can't see far right now, seeing his dark eyes look for my voice brings me more joy than I could ever imagine. At first I assumed his eyes were dark brown like Liam's, but they're actually a deep blue, nearing navy. I wish with all of my might that you'll be in my arms soon, sweet boy.

Hudson seemed more interested in *Oliver Gilmore, a Doxie's Diary*, and I think that means he's going to be a dog lover, and maybe enjoy travelling. Either that, or he hates my attempt at singing the song Oliver's dad sings to him in the book. Hudson's little eyes peek open for a moment, but not long enough for me to determine what colour they are. He's had an exhausting day and has earned his sleep.

Dola and Zara have both agreed to stay as long as they're needed, so each of the babies will have someone with them as much as possible. I want to be by their sides 24/7, but I know that's not possible while I recover. That doesn't make leaving them easy.

When I'm wheeled back to my room, I keep replaying the scene with Lenox lying in his cot with a tube coming out of his chest. I can't help but sob. For a few short hours, I thought everything would be okay. I thought I did something right for once in my life. I should have known better.

Isla is sitting in my room when I return, fiddling with her phone. She tucks it into the side pocket on her leggings, and I make a mental note to ask her where she got that genius article of clothing. "Sorry, I was just texting Rory. She was asking about the babies."

"Why are you sorry, silly? That's nice of her to ask." I sniffle, trying to get my emotions under control; something I haven't been successful at for a quarter of a century.

Isla seems unsure of what to say. "I didn't know what to tell her. How are they?"

It occurs to me that Isla only knows *something* was going on, but probably not *what*. I relay to her the events of the past two hours and her terrified expression does little to squash my own fears.

"Hopefully Liam will check in soon so we'll know how Lenox is getting settled. I hate I couldn't go with him."

"Chels, you just had a major surgery, and went from zero to three kids in a matter of minutes. You have to look after yourself, too. Right now, just let us all be here for you. All four of you need care and support, so as a family, we'll make sure you get it."

I stare at my little sister, who is wise beyond her years. She knows a thing or two about long-term hospital stays. "Thanks, Troublemaker. I know you have a lot going on with school starting soon, so don't worry about me. You can go home."

"Oh, no you don't. You're not getting rid of me. Reason one, Mom would strangle me. She was adamant that someone be here with you at all times. Reason two, like you said, school is starting soon. Not today."

I chuckle, imagining Zara issue her empty threats, which no one ever calls her on because it's sweet she gets so determined. I guess there's one thing I could use help with. "Want to grab the breast pump out of my bag and help me figure it out?"

For a split second, Isla looks to be deciding what's worse: not following through Zara's orders or helping me with a breast pump. Ultimately, she decides Zara is scarier.

The two of us sit in the hospital room, assembling this bright yellow, electric double breast pump. I did a lot of research online and this one seemed to be the best, but it sure comes with a lot of parts. I wasn't aware I'd need an engineering degree to build the thing first. You may not need to pass a test before procreating, but these baby-product manufacturers send things in as many parts as possible, making it a certainty you'll have to demonstrate patience, logic, and basic reading skills.

Liam returns to my room at 7pm. I fell asleep for about an hour, but sleeping in the maternity ward is difficult. Especially when you constantly hear babies crying and can't hold your own.

I perk up seeing his arrival but worry about what he'll say. "How's Lenox?"

"Babe, you should see him. They called him a big chubby baby, because he's in a room normally reserved for micro-preemies under a thousand grams. Can you believe that?" Liam's eyes drop as his moment of excitement disappears. "It's hard to see him like that, but it will help him grow big and strong. Do you want to see a picture?"

Do I want to see a picture? If Liam says it's hard seeing Lenox, I can't imagine how I'll handle it. But he's my baby, and I want to know everything that's happening. "Yeah, I do."

105

TIFFANY ANDREA

Liam slides onto the edge of the bed, pulling his phone from his back pocket. "I took some videos of him too. He's sedated, so he's going to wake up healthy and strong, with no memory of this."

When Liam pulls up the photo, I gasp. My baby is covered in wires, medical tape, tubes, and monitors. I ask Liam to explain what each thing was, and as I expected, Liam asked the doctors and nurses no less than eighty questions to make sure he knew what everything was for. They equipped Lenox with an umbilical catheter, several monitors to check oxygen levels and heart rate, and a ventilator. Seeing him there, sedated, helpless, and clinging to life, I lose every ounce of joy I had been feeling.

When Liam plays the video, Lenox's entire body is vibrating rapidly. I wasn't expecting that, so it shocks me even more. "What's happening to him?"

"They put him on this special ventilator. I guess because of the pneumothorax, this will help him heal better. I know it looks scary, Chels, but they know what they're doing. They're a well-oiled machine in there, and he has a nurse all to himself. They gave me this phone number for you, so you can call and ask how he's doing anytime, day or night."

I take the paperwork Liam hands me, tucking into the side of the mattress. "Did they say how long he'll be like that?"

"He'll be on this ventilator for a few days, but he could need several weeks in the hospital. Once he's more stable, they might be able to move all three babies to Orillia, or somewhere closer to home."

Several weeks. That means even once I'm discharged in a few days, I'll have to go home without our babies. Liam can't take that much time off work. Neither can Dola nor Zara. Isla is starting college soon, so I can't derail her future. The difficult reality of the weeks ahead hits me and the stress of the day takes over.

Liam lies back on the bed beside me, placing one arm around me. "Shh. Babe, it's going to be fine. While I was waiting for him to get transferred and settled in a room, I was reading NICU success stories in the hallway. They have a whole display board with letters from parents whose babies went through the same things. You'd probably bawl your eyes out reading them."

I chuckle. "Probably. Pregnancy hormones are no joke."

"Our babies are so lucky to have you. You know when I proposed, I said I hoped every day would be the best day of your life?" I nod as he wipes a falling tear from my face. "Today was the best day of my life, Chels. You've made me the luckiest guy on the planet. I can't even put into words how much I love you and our sons."

"We love you too. So much."

Breathe Easy

20

Six days have passed since the birth of our babies. They finally discharged me this morning after an extended stay on account of some issues surrounding my C-section incision, but I'm well enough now to leave, as long as I follow the doctor's strict orders. Even more exciting than being discharged, today is the first day I get to see all three of my babies. I've been spending every moment with Lincoln and Hudson, but it pained me to not be able to see Lenox.

Becoming a NICU parent means joining a club you never wanted to be a part of. Lying in my hospital bed for six days, listening to other newborn babies cry and their mothers being able to tend to them, comfort them, love them, it filled me with a jealousy I hate myself for. I shouldn't feel envious of others having healthy babies, but I do.

Since delivering our boys, I haven't been able to hold any of them. In addition to everything else, they're under phototherapy lights being treated for jaundice. My only saving grace is that the nurses and doctors give more love and attention to the babies than they do medicine. Walking away from our children each time feels like the longest, most draining walk of my life, and it never gets easier; but today is different. Today, after our visits, I'll be heading home, and I don't know how I'm supposed to leave the building without my babies.

When Liam wheels me into the *SickKids* NICU ward, we stop in the waiting room where he uses the intercom to call reception and wait for the all clear to enter the room Lenox is in. There are six babies in each room, so if another baby is having a procedure or if the doctor's rounds are going through, they ask you to wait outside for privacy reasons.

In the waiting room, I strike up a conversation with another woman whose son has been in the NICU for eight weeks. When she describes the turmoil they've been through, I feel bad for whining about our situation. Her son was born at twenty-six weeks, weighing less than a kilo, and had to undergo surgery on his intestines, which he barely survived.

I desperately want to give her a hug and tell her everything will be okay, but those are just words. Words I can't guarantee. When it's your child's life on the line, nothing a stranger says or does can ease the pain. All I do is reach my hand out to grab hers atop her bouncing knee and say, "just keep loving him."

At that moment, the receptionist announces on the intercom that we're able to enter Lenox's room, and as excited as I am to see him, I feel guilty about leaving this grieving mother. She must sense my hesitation because she flips her hand over to squeeze mine and says, "go see your baby."

Liam and I say goodbye and he wheels me into room two. The room is large, sterile—thankfully—and full of quiet commotion. Machines beep. Nurses are methodically moving around, filling out charts, and examining their charges. Liam pushes me to the end cot on the left and parks me beside our baby boy. He scored a window seat.

He's back on the regular ventilator and making progress, based on what I've been told during my many phone calls and Liam's detailed daily reports. The large IV machine has three bags of medication attached. Liam has explained everything to me beforehand, so I'm not surprised. For what I think is the first time, I'm grateful for Liam's incessant question asking. Lenox has a nasogastric tube in place to feed him, and the heart-shaped medical tape on his face holding it in place makes me smile. Little things in a sea of big ones can make all the difference—proven by all the tiny humans in this room.

"Hi, baby boy. It's Mommy." I reach my hand into his bed, finding his, and stroking it gently. His fingers wrap around my index finger, which startles me. "He grabbed my finger. I thought he was sedated."

The nurse introduces herself after hearing my question. Her name is Kate, and she has a student nurse named Fallon shadowing her. I smile, thinking our baby is lucky to have two people at his beck and call. Kate is petite, with short dark hair and a friendly smile. Fallon is a tall blonde, and probably could have landed on the cover of a magazine had she chosen a different career.

Kate responds to my comment. "He is sedated, but certain instincts will still kick in." She looks at Liam, then at me with a wide smile. "I see Lenox got his looks from his mommy. I think he's happy to see you."

I stare at my little red-headed boy, smiling, and feeling closer to whole again. Kate and Fallon continue to explain, in great detail, the care Lenox has received over the past few days. He's been fed through his nasogastric tube and given a soother at the same time, so he associates sucking with feeling full. He required a few x-rays to check on his chest and ensure everything was in place after his lung collapsed. The air that collected in his chest cavity compressed his heart, resulting in a slight heart murmur, but they assure me it should resolve itself as he grows.

Despite the rough road, he is doing phenomenal, and they're hoping to wean him off the sedation in a day or two. That also means taking him off the ventilator, and then they'll be able to remove the umbilical line. Once that's removed, we'll be able to hold him for the first time.

It's tough to accept that our baby, who has been a part of me for seven months, has gone days without feeling a warm embrace. The only touches he's received are those of needles, monitors, and diaper changes. I can't wait to hold him in my arms and tell him how much he's loved.

I sit at his bedside for three hours, talking to him, telling him about his brothers and his family, and Liam and I read several books to him. He squeezes my finger a little tighter when we read *Spike, the Penguin With Rainbow Hair*, and it makes me giggle. Our little penguin has colourful hair too.

At 6:45pm Liam informs me we have to leave while the nurses' shifts change so they can relay any pertinent information to their replacements. I'm not ready to leave Lenox, but I'm not sure I ever will be.

When I try to pull my hand away, even though my arm is asleep after being in the same position for hours, I feel a little squeeze of my finger. My eyes shoot to Liam. "He doesn't want to let me go. I can't leave him."

With his eyes downcast, Liam reminds me, "Babe, we have to give the nurses space to get organized."

Of course, I know that. But that doesn't make leaving any less hard. When Lenox relaxes his grip, I pull my hand away, allowing the blood to flow in my arm again. I stand just enough to kiss my hand and place it on his back. He's still susceptible to sickness, so I want to be cautious, but there's nothing I want more than to let him know how much I love him.

We make our way past the waiting room, where I glance to see if the lady from earlier is around, but she's not. I hope that means she's by her baby's bedside and received some good news today. I feel a solidarity with her and want her to hold her baby as much as I want to hold my own.

Travelling through the tunnel connecting *SickKids* to *Mount Sinai*, Liam is chatting about any random thing that comes to mind. I issue the odd, "uh-huh," or, "that's nice," but my mind is elsewhere. I'm daydreaming about what life will be like when we have three babies under one roof, not having to worry about their oxygen saturation, heart rates, or CO2 scores.

The nurses are switching shifts at *Mount Sinai* as well, so Liam takes me to *BarBurrito* in the hospital food court. A *super* romantic date experience, sitting in the hospital's lobby, patients being wheeled by with IVs attached, while I'm in my own wheelchair, wearing an oversized sundress, a pair of hospital issued mesh underwear, and a maxi-pad the size of Manhattan. Everything about the scenario is the antithesis of romance. Even so, having time alone with Liam is nice in any shape or form.

Shoveling down the last bites of my bean, cheese, and guacamole bowl, Liam crinkles his burrito wrapper into a ball and pushes his chair out to stand. "Shall we go see our boys?"

"Yes, please."

Since I need to walk short distances, we ditch the wheelchair and walk hand-in-hand to the NICU—a journey that gives me great anxiety after coming in to find Lenox being tended to six days earlier. My first sight is one that brings me tears of joy instead of fear. Hudson is breathing on his own. Not aided by oxygen—breathing room air like a champion.

"Are you ready to hold your baby?" the nurse asks, beaming at both Liam and me. Seeing Hudson with one less tube on him makes me happy but being able to hold him in my arms for the first time is the best news we've had in days.

Liam insists I hold him first, and the nurse pulls up a wooden rocking chair with floral cushions. It's a stark contrast to the sterility of the room, but a welcome bit of hominess. Nurse Nazleen places Hudson in my arms, and I couldn't tell you anything happening around me, because all I can do is stare at my sweet baby boy. I discovered two days ago that he has deep brown eyes like his daddy. His skin is getting darker too, looking like he's gotten sun-kissed, and he's shed a little of his body hair, but not much. Our little dog lover is still obsessed with Oliver Gilmore, and he perks up each time I read it.

I've been told skin-to-skin contact is beneficial for newborns, so with some fancy finagling, Nazleen helps me position my furry child on my chest, and I hold him with one hand while I read him his favourite book. He doesn't have any control of his head or neck, but he's attempting to follow my voice. With countless medical staff and visitors over the last six days, I wasn't sure he'd know my voice from anyone else. Among my other fears, I was worried the excessive number of people around our boys would impact our ability to bond, but seeing Hudson attempt to look up at me as I read is all the reassurance I need. He knows I'm his mom. I've never felt more valued or needed in my entire life.

Liam snaps a few photos commemorating when I held our son for the first time, and the look of pure happiness on his face mirrors my own. I could stay here forever under this tiny, hairy baby boy and be content.

My life, thus far, has been marked with one challenge after another. One mistake, followed by the next. One trauma piled on top of previous ones. None of that matters right now. Sure, it's shaped who I am, and will always be a part of me, but the only thing that matters is my family. I will do everything in my power to make sure history never repeats itself.

I tilt my head down, placing a gentle kiss on Hudson's head. They will not be the carriers of my generational curse.

A Sight for Sore Eyes

21

Liam places our coffee order, making obligatory small talk with the woman on the other side of the counter.

When I hear her say, "You guys are so lucky you've been able to go home and sleep every night," I stand in place, staring at the well-meaning stranger who is oblivious to the turmoil and difficulties of having babies in the NICU.

Anyone who thinks I'm sleeping all night is mistaken. I barely sleep because I spend my nights anxious over whether they are okay in my absence. Are they crying? Are they in some sort of medical distress and I have no idea? Again. Are they bonding with the nurses who have been tasked with caring for them and been more present in their lives than I have?

Not to mention waking every three hours to attach myself to my trusty Medela breast pump.

Sleep is definitely not on the agenda. It's on a wish list.

"Soooo lucky that our kids couldn't breathe on their own and required medical intervention." Liam's response is marked with an uncharacteristic ridicule. My eyes shift to the right to look at him, but his face is intent on the meddling barista who last saw me thirty-one weeks pregnant.

Without another word, he walks down to the end of the counter, waiting to pick up our overpriced caffeinated beverages. Before following suit, I send the woman an apologetic look, knowing she doesn't understand our situation, nor do I ever want her to. She stares back at me with a blank look, unsure of what to say, so I walk away with no more words exchanged.

"I can't believe some people can be so ignorant!"

I study my husband, who is not one to get his feathers ruffled easily, but her comment has got him in a huff.

"Some people just don't know. Do you think you would have understood how hard it is until we experienced it?"

He stares down at the floor with a sheepish expression. "No, I guess not." Another server places our drinks on the counter and Liam passes mine to me. "Give me a second." He walks back to the cash register where we placed our order and the barista looks as if she wants to duck behind the counter. I feel the need to step in between them, not knowing what Liam's intentions are, but I know him and assume they aren't nefarious. "I'm sorry for snapping at you. I... We've just been stressed and tired."

"No, I'm sorry. I didn't consider how hard it would be." She fiddles with her nametag, which states her name is Rachel. "I have two kids of my own, and I was exhausted when they were newborns, but I can't imagine not having them home. I really am sorry."

Liam nods and drops a ten-dollar bill into the tip jar before turning back to me and grabbing my hand to walk out the door.

I've learned over the years that many people are unintentionally ignorant of things they haven't experienced themselves. It's usually things no one would wish on another

116

human, so helping them to understand with civil conversation is the best way. I'm proud of Liam for humbling himself to apologize. This man is everything I never imagined possible in a husband and father of my children. I look up at him with a smile on my face and he leads me to our new Toyota Sienna minivan to shuttle us home.

After or coffee date, Liam had to go to work for a few hours. It turns out they're not very amenable to him taking several weeks off with a takeover looming, but that hasn't been Liam's chief concern. He's tried to pacify them as long as he could, working from home, or even from the hospital, but he's needed in the office.

I'm still recovering, so I don't want to drive to Toronto myself. I'll wait for him to return from work, and we can drive down together to spend a few hours with the boys. Dola and Ian offered to go spend time with them this morning, so I'm pleased they'll have family around.

A knock at the door startles me while I'm in the kitchen making lunch. I never know who to expect when people show up without notice, so I creep to the door, trying to determine who's on the other side. It's a good thing Liam and I went out for coffee this morning, or I still would have been in my pyjamas.

The solitary figure is low on the list of who I would have guessed. "Fred?"

"Hiya, Chels. Do you have a minute?"

My brain churns out a hundred possibilities why Zara's father is at my door. He's been here a handful of times, but never without Alanna at his side. "Sure. Come on in. I'm sorry for the mess."

"Looks good to me." He slides off his shoes before walking into my kitchen.

"Can I get you something? I was just making lunch. Or would you like coffee?"

"Um. No thanks. I'm sorry for dropping in on you like this, but I have some news."

Ambiguous statements like that are a guaranteed method for amplifying anxiety, a never-ending side effect of PTSD.

"What kind of news?"

Fred blows out a breath, running his hand across his balding head. He's kept himself in excellent shape since retiring as a firefighter, but his hair, or lack thereof, shows his age. "Your father... your father died."

For a moment, I have to fight to stay upright, assuming he is talking about Zach. He's the only father figure I've ever really had, but then relief hits as I understand who he's referring to. "Kevin? He's dead?"

"I'm afraid so. Turns out he had prostate cancer, and he died yesterday."

I'm afraid so? Like this is a substantial loss to humanity? Nah. Good riddance. I hope his death was long and painful, like my childhood.

What is wrong with me? My father, despite his failings as a parent, still gave me life. Am I a monster for being relieved he's gone? Is his heartlessness genetic? Will I fail my own children the way he failed me?

A flood of emotions I wasn't expecting tears through me and before I know it, I lean over the counter, sobbing into my hands. I hear a stool sliding across the floor before I'm pulled into a comforting hug.

"Let it out," he says while stroking the back of my head and pulling me into his chest. "I'm sorry, Chels. I know you don't need this right now. My buddy at the police station called to let me know and asked if I wanted to be the one to tell you. I hated the thought of a stranger coming here and opening old wounds."

I shake my head, not wanting Fred to feel an ounce of guilt over the situation. "It's not the fact he's dead that bothers me. What scares me is how happy I feel about it. I'm a monster."

"You are not a monster." He tilts my face, so he's looking into my eyes. "Look at me. That man deserved what life handed him. Three meals a day and a bed to sleep in were too good for him, and I, for one, hope he suffered. Does that make me a monster?"

I contemplate his words, wondering when Fred developed such a hatred for Kevin, because he's never once expressed it before. I assumed he was Switzerland on the matter. "No, I don't think you're a monster."

"If it makes you feel any better, I spent many nights fantasizing about ending his life myself after what he'd done to you. I'm only sorry I didn't get the chance."

His words have taken me by complete surprise. I've always viewed Fred as the sweet, kindly grandfather who dedicated his career to saving lives. Hearing him confess his desire to take one has me dumbfounded. Yet, I don't view him as evil for having those thoughts.

He pulls me into another hug, and after a moment, places a hand on either of my shoulders, squaring me to face him again. "You're free, Chels. He can never hurt you again."

I give Fred a one-sided smile, unsure how to proceed. How do you grieve someone who sought to destroy your value as a human? Do I grieve, or is it okay to celebrate being free?

When Liam returns home from work, he finds me drinking wine; something I haven't done since before we started dating. To me, alcohol was the gateway to a slippery slope into cocaine addiction. Today, I need it.

I can see Liam staring at me from my peripheral vision, but I'm refusing to look at him.

"Babe? Are you okay? I thought we were going to see the boys."

"My *father* died yesterday." I say the word with as much disdain as I can, so Liam doesn't have the same panic I did, thinking it was Zach.

Liam sits on the sofa beside me, pulling me toward him. "Are you okay?"

I nod, staring into my near empty wineglass. "That's the problem. Fred came over to tell me today, and I was happy." I down the last of my pino noir. "Happy Liam. The man is dead, and I wanted to smile. What's wrong with me?"

He doesn't reply right away, allowing a few seconds to pass. "Chels, what he did to you... all of it... was awful. Awful isn't even the right word, but I don't know how else to describe it. Nobody should ever go through those things, especially not at the hands of their parent. So, he may have contributed to your DNA, and for that I thank him, but beyond that, the world is better off without him. I'm only sorry I didn't get to take care of him myself."

I chuckle. "That's what Fred said." I turn to face Liam, who is staring at my empty wineglass. "I guess I was right."

"About what?"

"Being a terrible parent is genetic. The first hard thing to come my way and I contaminate our children's food supply."

He stands up from the couch, grabbing my wine glass and carrying it toward the kitchen. To my surprise, he fills it up again. "Babe, this is not the first hard thing to come your way. You're forgetting the long line of hard things we've been living through for months. This is just what tipped the scales. So, you've earned this." Returning to my perch on the sofa, he passes me the glass. "Drink up while I go change, then you can pump and dump on the drive."

I look at him with a cocked brow. "Pump and dump?"

He shrugs. "I was reading BabyCenter forums while I was at work." He laughs, and I fall in love with the sound that's become few and far between over the past few weeks. "Let's go see our babies."

Breast Friend

22

I know how cows feel. I've spent more time with my breast pump than I have with Liam over the past two weeks. He joked he was going to sell me to Starbucks because I could supply a single location with enough milk for their daily quota. He thought it was funny. I did not.

My determination to do what's best for our babies keeps me waking up every three hours to attach myself to the torture device that extracts my children's food.

Dr. Seuss could have written a book about me and my breast pump. *I can pump from dusk 'til dawn, in the car with my seatbelt on. I can pump inside my home, at the mall, and while I roam. Even when my boobs are floppy, no one else will ever stop me.*

This is a skill I never imagined I'd need. Yet, here I am, flipping pancakes, collecting milk. I hate it, but I'm happy to do it. I want to stop, but I'm determined to keep going. I'm exhausted, but I'd sacrifice any amount of sleep to make sure my kids have the best I can give them.

"I'm getting jealous of that thing." Liam walks into the kitchen, pulling his grey t-shirt over his head. I sneak a peek at his torso and feel a surge of disgust, knowing how mine currently looks.

"If it's any consolation, I'm making your food too." I roll my eyes. Maybe I can sabotage his figure by feeding him loads of refined carbs. It might make me feel better about the condition of my own.

He walks over to give me a kiss and pours himself a coffee. "Are you ready for today?"

How do I answer that? Today Lincoln and Hudson are being moved to *Soldiers Memorial Hospital* in Orillia. They're stable enough to be downgraded to a level two NICU. That's great, and I'm happy they'll be closer to home, but it also means our time now has to be divided not just between three babies in two hospitals, but two different cities.

"I guess. I'm just worried about how we'll balance our time between them. I hate that Lenox is being left behind."

"I know, but he'll be transferred soon. You heard what they said yesterday. He's doing well on oxygen, so it should only be a couple of days before he joins his big brothers. We're in the final stretch. They're coming home soon." He wraps his arms around me from behind, which is an awkward position given that I'm wearing a hands-free nursing bra, trying to flip pancakes, but I still welcome his embrace.

"Not soon enough." I switch the stove off and turn so I can see Liam from the corner of my eye. I give a little wiggle and ask, "want some milk for your coffee?"

He lets out a throaty laugh. "You're crazy. But I love every crazy thing about you."

"I love you, too."

By 11:30am, I'm standing over Lenox's cot, staring at my five-pound baby boy. He's grown so much in the past four weeks, yet he's still a tiny guy. Looking around the room, I see how small some of the micro preemies are, and my stomach knots knowing the battles they're going to face, having to grow outside the safety of their mother's tummy.

"How's momma today?" Kate chimes in, multi-tasking by checking various equipment and monitors and recording information on Lenox's chart.

"I'm okay, thanks. I was just thinking about how big Lenox has gotten since he was born. He really looks like the big chubby baby."

Kate giggles. "He is big compared to most we have here. When he first arrived I had to go to the room next door to find diapers big enough."

My son clocked in at just over three pounds and fourteen inches when he arrived here a month ago. His neighbour directly across from his bed, a baby girl, Anya, was born at twenty-five weeks, and has been here for four months already. She still has a long road ahead. Just the other day, we rejoiced with her parents as she topped six pounds, because she was born weighing less than two. A fresh wave of guilt crashes through me when I think of the toll the last four months have taken on Anya's parents.

"I feel bad that I complained about not seeing Lenox for a few days, when, looking around, other babies and parents have it so much worse."

Kate studies me for a second, hanging the chart back on the end of Lenox's cot. "Just because your stay here has been easier than some doesn't mean it hasn't been hard. Don't discount your own trauma because someone else's was different. Yours is still valid."

Kate's words hit me in more ways than one. I've discounted my trauma for a lot of my life, knowing it was awful, but also knowing many people aren't spared the horrors of human trafficking or parental neglect or abuse. I thought I was lucky I escaped that. I thought I was fortunate we're going to walk out of here with three healthy babies one day, because a lot of parents don't have that privilege. But, despite the way things turned out, Kate's right. My trauma is still valid. As much as I don't want Kevin to control my life, the effects of my childhood will impact me for the rest of it. Trying to minimize the impact it's had is only causing it to fester. Like a raging infection, you can't just ignore it and hope it goes away. It has to be dealt with.

"Thank you, Kate." She hands Lenox to me and the tears of joy trickling down my face are the sweetest tears I've ever cried. Not that holding the other two is any less sweet, but Lenox has overcome more odds than anyone, so holding him feels like the light at the end of the tunnel.

I stare at my baby boy, aware that he has his late grandfather's flaming orange hair, but for the first time in my life I have love for it, rather than resentment. I'm no longer going to be held prisoner by fear of my father that couldn't be suppressed, even when he was on the other side of a jail cell. I'm going to dedicate my life to loving my boys the way I needed to be loved.

A short time later, we see Hudson and Lincoln off in their transports to *Soldiers Memorial*, and go back to Lenox's bedside. I hear a familiar voice behind me. "Looks like the big guy is getting sprung tomorrow morning. There's a transport set up to take him to Orillia when the next shift ends." Kate looks excited by the news and seeing the pride in her face makes me appreciate her so much more. She didn't just come to do a job. Her role in our lives has been short, but more impactful than she'll ever know.

"That's great. He can finally be back with his brothers," Liam adds.

I'm choked up, unable to speak.

"We're at capacity here, so I'm happy he's graduating. The next nurse on duty will ride with him to get him set up at the hospital and relay his information, but aside from that, his next move should be home."

I finally find my ability to speak without crying. "We can't thank you guys enough. Honestly. There's nothing in the world we could do to express what the care you've given Lenox means to us. I'm kind of sad we're leaving because I know he's in such good hands here, but if him moving because he's strong enough means another baby who isn't gets the attention they need, then I'm happy to make room for them."

"You guys have been a pleasure. I've loved caring for Lenox, and I'm happy you guys are one step closer to having your boys home."

When Liam and I leave the NICU a few hours later, I feel sad knowing I'll probably never see these men and women who cared for my son again. I'll never be able to repay them for all they've done, but I'll never take their sacrifices for granted. These angels on Earth will forever have a place in our hearts.

Don't Miss a Beat

23

I f I blink, they might disappear. I can't believe this is real. All three of our boys under our roof. Our house finally feels like a home.

Liam had the nursery finished while I was still in the hospital, thanks to Zach, Isla, Fred, and Alanna. Three white cribs are lined up along a charcoal-grey accent wall with a realistic New York City skyline painted by hand. Isla's artistic talents came through beautifully, featuring the *One World Trade Center* and the other beautiful architecture Liam and I fell in love with. The boys each have white bedding, but different blankets, which was an intentional decision to give them a bit of individuality. We don't want them to spend their lives being known as "the triplets." We want them to be Lenox, Lincoln, and Hudson.

We have a change table next to the sofa under the window dressed with yellow curtains, and two dressers to accommodate the 197 onesies and sleepers that are required when you have three infants. The finishing touches were added by a yellow and white chevron carpet, and a crystal light-fixture that creates fractals of light bouncing off of every surface. We struggled to settle on a style, but I think the New York City theme is absolutely perfect.

When I assumed we wouldn't worry about oxygen saturation, heart rates, or CO2 scores when we came home, I was wrong. Instead of feeling confident that our babies are healthy enough to *be* at home, I lie awake staring at them, afraid to fall asleep because we no longer have alarms to alert us if something goes wrong. Liam keeps trying to convince me to come to bed, but I've been power napping on the sofa in the boys' room since they arrived home two weeks ago.

Yes, I'm tired. I want to sleep, but I can't shut my brain off to allow that to happen. I can't deactivate my worry mode, and I don't know how I'm meant to survive like this. I'm so afraid a moment away from them will make them feel neglected, and I will not allow that to happen.

Dola interrupts my vacant stare at our three beautiful sleeping babies. "Hi, Love." I turn to face her, but before I can say anything she continues, "I'm here to relieve you so you can sleep."

She's waiting for me to respond, but I'm so drowsy, my movements mimic a sloth; they have no excuse to move so slowly though. They sleep twenty hours a day. I haven't slept twenty hours in the last five days combined.

"Did Liam call you?"

"He did, but I wanted to come see my grandbabies, anyway. So don't argue with me. Go upstairs and sleep in the guest room so you won't hear us, and if I need you, I'll come get you."

I look back at the boys, not wanting to leave them. I'm afraid if I leave, something will go wrong. Dola is far more equipped to handle anything than I am, but there's a biological need for me to be close to them. We lost so much time with them in the hospital; I want to soak up every minute now. Today is my official due date, and in the time they should have been growing inside of me, I feel I've missed out on so much.

"I'm not taking no for an answer, Love. Get yourself upstairs. Have a shower, get some sleep. We'll be fine. I even called Zara on my way over, and she's coming shortly."

How am I to argue with that? Two doting grandmothers want to have some time with their grandsons; I would be horrible to not allow it.

"Okay. Thank you for this. I'll just sleep for a little while because they'll all want to eat when they wake up. Just wake me if I don't get up on my own."

I blow each boy a kiss and make my way upstairs to our guest room. The room has been neglected over the past few months, with the once pristine decor being mixed with baby gear and boxes of diapers in every brand and size. It does little for the aesthetic of the space. Regardless, I'm going to rest my head and attempt to shut my brain off long enough to sleep. I assume it won't be easy, but my body disagrees.

When I wake up, I take a few seconds to adjust to my surroundings. I haven't woken anywhere but the sofa in the boys' room since they returned home; this space feels foreign. I hear voices downstairs, so I stop in the bathroom before heading to the family room.

I'm greeted by the smiling faces of Zara, Isla, and Dola, each with a baby in their arms.

"Sleeping Beauty is finally awake," Zara states.

I look into the kitchen at the clock on the stove to notice it's 4:39pm. I rub my eyes, certain I'm seeing it wrong. I went upstairs at 10:20am. For a nap. A siesta. Not a six-hour snooze. That explains why my boobs hurt so much. "Why didn't anyone wake me? I should have been up to feed the boys."

"Chels, relax. Everything is under control. They've eaten, and they are content. You needed sleep." Zara shrugs, glancing at Dola, who is seated on our navy sofa with Lincoln.

"She's right, Love. Rest is necessary, and we've all had a wonderful time with the babies. It takes a village."

I want to appreciate their help, their generosity, but all I feel is guilt. Remorse for the fact other people are here caring for children I brought into the world. Shame for having them spend weeks being tended to by strangers who were providing things I couldn't just to keep them alive. Regret that I've missed out on the last six hours with them after being absent for so many already. I can't rewind the clock, but I can't remove the self-condemnation with logic either.

"I'm so sorry. I didn't mean to sleep that long." I slept longer than I have in weeks—months, probably—but I still feel tired. Tired and guilty.

"We were just talking about how amazing it is that the first time you got pregnant, you had three babies at once. The odds must be one in a million. You should play the lottery." Isla is smirking at me, one finger tucked in Lenox's fist.

I don't know how to respond to her because it wasn't my first pregnancy. More guilt is piled on knowing I've kept Sugar a secret from everyone just to shield them from the hurt. That's done nothing but deny our first baby's existence.

"Actually, I was pregnant once before." Silence. Two shocked faces peer back at me, but neither speaks. Dola was in the know thanks to Liam, so it's not a surprise to her. Still, I don't want Zara to think I told my mother-in-law over her, so I address all three of them. "I was pregnant last summer and wanted to wait until twelve weeks to tell everyone. You know, they say 'wait until you're out of the danger zone.'" I add a head wobble for emphasis, so they know that's a real thing "experts" say. "But at our first ultrasound, around eleven weeks, we found out the baby died. A baby we ended up naming Sugar since that seemed like a cute gender-neutral name and Sugar Hill was our favourite area in Manhattan." I'm rambling now, looking at my hands wringing together in my lap.

"Oh, Chels. I wish you would have told us. I'm so sorry you went through that on your own." Zara lays Hudson on a blanket on the floor and walks over to sit beside me on the couch, wrapping her left arm around me.

"It's fine. There's nothing you could have done to change it." I sniffle, wiping a singular tear from my cheek.

"We may not have been able to change the reality, but we could have been a support team. We could have at least loved you."

I stand from my seat, sliding out from Zara's arm, and return a moment later holding a folded piece of paper dated October 13. I hand it to Zara, who opens it to view the contents.

"Sugar." She looks up at me, wide-eyed. "You guys wrote your baby a letter?"

I nod. "It was our way of saying goodbye."

She reads the letter out loud, and by the end of it, aside from the babies, there's not a dry eye in the house.

"Oh, Chels. That is beautiful. It's such a lovely tribute to your first baby." Zara folds the paper and sets it on the end table. "I know it doesn't make the loss any easier, but Hudson, Lincoln, and Lenox, well, they exist because Sugar doesn't. And from now on—now that we know—Sugar will always be remembered as a part of our family, but I'm grateful for the three beautiful babies you have here."

I've come to that conclusion before. That reality was never lost on me, that if I was still pregnant with Sugar, I would have never become pregnant with the boys. And having them here, I couldn't imagine an alternate reality. Zara is right. Sugar deserves to be remembered as part of our family, but I can't allow the fear and sadness that came as a result of our loss to dictate how I love our boys going forward.

Follow Your Heart

24

'm tired; operating with my energy tank on empty. The little bits of sleep I get do little to quell my drowsiness. Looking at my reflection, the bags under my eyes appear to extend down to my jawline. I'm just a walking, talking, epitome of exhaustion. I could walk into a high school class right now and convince them to remain abstinent just by my appearance alone.

Today Isla and her friend Rory are coming to spend some time with the babies, and I'm looking forward to some adult interaction. In the two months since the boys have been home, the weather has morphed from comfortable outdoor temperatures and changing leaves to bitterly cold, snow-covered, and unpredictable. Needless to say, taking three infants out on my own isn't a frequent occurrence. I need an extra set of hands to go anywhere and gone are the days of "running to the store." Every trip outside these walls requires enough gear to stock Babies 'R' Us. It's fine when Liam is home, but when I'm here alone, it can be overwhelming.

There is a gentle knock on the door, which I barely hear, so I walk over after placing Hudson in his baby swing. I'll have to look up whoever invented those and send them a thank-you card.

"Hey, girls. Come in."

"I didn't want to ring the bell in case anyone was sleeping," red-cheeked Isla says as she steps through the door and gives me a hug. Her puffy, down-filled coat feels cold, and I'm pleased I have a legitimate excuse to stay inside.

"Thank you for that. Everyone is wide awake, though. Waiting for their auntie time." I greet Rory and give them a moment to remove their extensive amount of outdoor clothing and walk back over to where I left the boys.

Lenox is fussing because I have him down for tummy-time and he's not a fan. Rory parks herself on the floor with him and does an incredible job eliciting a few smiles. She sings to them every time she comes over and if I didn't know better, I'd think my little charmers have a crush.

Isla strikes up a conversation with Lincoln in the bouncy chair before she looks up at me. "Why don't you go get some sleep? We'll wake you if we need anything."

The guilt that usually accompanies these offers is nowhere to be found today. I'm too tired to feel bad about pawning my kids off. "Do I look that bad?" I chuckle.

"You look tired. We have nothing else to do today, so go sleep, shower, and when you wake up, we can still hang out for a while."

She is singing my song. That's everything I wanted to hear in one sentence. Sleep. Shower. Adult conversation.

"Come get me if you need me." I walk into my bedroom, this time without a second thought. I lie on the bed and drift off to sleep.

133

After I've showered a few hours later, I find myself dawdling, not rushing to get back to the boys. It's not lost on me that just a few weeks ago, I would have refused a few hours of sleep and rushed through a shower just so I didn't miss a minute with them. But, in that time, I've realized that my love for them is not shown merely in the time I dedicate to them. There's much to be said for quality over quantity, and it's better for them to have less of a rested mom than more of a tired one.

We're so fortunate to have such a loving family, all of whom are willing to come help whenever their schedules permit. Isla has been an integral part of our childcare team and comes over as often as possible. Zara still comes at least once a week to help catch up with housework and spend time with the boys. For a woman who never had infants, she is a natural. Dola stops in several times a week and having a doctor in the family does wonders for aiding my medical anxiety regarding the boys. It's easy to ask a simple question, rather than haul them in for unnecessary appointments.

I return to find Isla, Rory, and Liam sitting in the family room, surrounded by various baby gear.

"Hey, Babe. Feel better?"

I walk over to give him a peck and smooth Hudson's dark hair as he's cradled in Liam's arms. "Much better. Thanks to these two."

Isla and Rory both give me a smile, but say nothing and continue to play with Lenox and Lincoln. All three boys are over ten pounds now and growing like little weeds. Lenox is still smaller and looks like an outcast among his near-identical brothers, but together they are three-quarters of my world.

A knock at the door startles me, and since I'm the only one without a baby, I walk over to answer. On the other side are Zara and Zach, beaming, carrying large bags of groceries.

"Hey! I didn't know you two were coming."

"Isla called earlier and said you could use a home-cooked meal tonight, so we figured we'd make a night of it, if that's okay."

"Of course. Wow, you guys brought a feast."

"We've got a lot of mouths to feed, and then you can have leftovers." Zara replies.

I look back in the house at the family whose loyalty and love has never wavered; I grew up not knowing that was possible. But something is missing. "Is there enough for me to call Dola and Ian too?"

Zara smiles, reaching out to pull me in for a tight squeeze. A gesture that used to overwhelm me with fear now feels like comfort.

"Of course. That would be great. We'll have a whole family dinner."

Whole. The idea of being whole after feeling empty and unworthy for so long. It's nice. Really nice.

Our dinner is pushed late, since Dola doesn't get off her shift at the clinic until six, but she wouldn't hear of postponing until another night. Zara, Zach, Isla, Rory, Liam, my three beautiful boys and I sit around a fire, taking turns snuggling babies, bottle feeding, playing peek-a-boo, and jingling keys.

Babies make life infinitely more complicated. Exhausting. Terrifying. But, they also make it so simple. Being content with the necessities of life, food, clothing, shelter; sometimes do away with clothing entirely. And love.

I love my sons more than I ever knew was humanly possible. I know now that love was not a feeling my biological father was capable of. Monsters don't love. They manipulate, use, betray. I am not him, and my journey will be a stark contrast to his.

When my time on this Earth is up, the people I love will surround me, and I'll know, despite the times I failed or made mistakes, I loved with every fibre of my being.

My parents work together in an awe-inspiring unified cooking session, preparing several dishes at once, communicating wordlessly with each other. The house smells amazing, and laughter fills the air. The fire crackles, and my babies smile. I soak it in, knowing exactly where I came from. From the pits of hell, I crawled out, suffered, struggled, and now I'm here.

"You look lost in thought. Are you okay?" Liam leans toward me on the sofa, wrapping his arm behind my shoulders.

"I'm good. Great actually. I'm just... happy."

Squeezing me a little tighter, Liam replies, "me too, Babe. Me too."

A knock at the door has Liam giving me a quick kiss, then runs off to open it, knowing it's his parents on the other side. I follow behind, seeing the kids are in good hands with Isla and Rory.

"Hi, Love. Thanks for inviting us." Dola greets me as she leans out of her heavy winter coat.

"It was all Mom and Dad. They brought food and have done the cooking. I can't take any credit, but we're glad you could make it."

Once everyone is inside, we get the babies settled for a nap in their bedroom—which is becoming a rarity to have them sleep at the same time during the day, or night—we sit around the ten-person table I thought was excessive when we purchased it. We've filled it up nicely.

The next hour passes as we converse over a feast, enjoying each other's company, and appreciating the differences we bring to the table. Literally. Isla, the quiet, creative type. Dola, the social-butterfly doctor. Rory, the shy musician. Zara, the fierce giver of life advice. Zach, the tender-hearted romantic. Ian, the intelligent gentleman. Liam, my reason for living.

And me. The luckiest woman in the entire world.

The odds of having triplets are around one in 10,000, which isn't as rare as I thought, but I had none of the underlying "risk" factors, making my odds significantly lower. Having them home with us, I feel like every pain in my life has led me to here, and I'd do it all over again if I knew it would turn out the same way.

I'll always battle my demons. My past will always be a part of me. But each moment with my family, with my boys, it gives me hope everything will be okay. It makes me feel like the pain was all worth it.

It doesn't matter how broken, overwhelmed, guarded, tired, or scared we are at any given time. We have each other no matter what, and I'll always keep loving them.

Love is the goal.

THE END

If you enjoyed Chelsea's story, please consider leaving a review on Amazon and/or Goodreads. Your reviews help give me feedback so I can continue to learn, and also helps my books garner more attention from other readers. I would greatly appreciate your thoughts!

To easily access links to my books, visit linktr.ee/burdenofproofreading. You can also sign up for my newsletter and find my social media links there.

Thank you health heroes!

Thank you, my darling girl, Amaya – SickKids NICU grad, 2010

Acknowledgements

Thank you doesn't seem like it will ever be enough. I continue to say thank you, but it doesn't convey how thankful I really am; to the medical staff who saved our daughter's life; to our friends and family who supported us through that time, and ever since; to my dear writing community full of talented authors who have encouraged me along this journey; and to each person who purchased a copy of this book.

Thank you.

To my husband and children, your support and encouragement through this process means everything to me. I'll never understand how I got so lucky to share my life with the three of you. I love you all more than words can express.

Special Thanks

F irst, I need to thank a very special human whom I have come to adore over the past many months, Carly. Your input in this book was wonderful, and I am grateful to you for sharing your time and love for children's books with me.

You may have noticed I mentioned three specific children's books in the story. I encourage you to read each of them, especially if you have young children, as they each have such sweet messages.

Spike: The Penguin With Rainbow Hair, written by Sarah Cullen and Carmen Ellis, illustrated by Zuzana Svobodova.

Do Not Wish For A Pet Ostrich!, written by Sarina Siebenaler, illustrated by Gabby Correia.

Oliver Gilmore: A Doxie's Diary, written by Greg McGoon, illustrated by Dave Reed.

Thank you to Sarah, Carmen, Sarina, and Greg for allowing me to include your books in this story.

Also, a special thank you to my advance readers for taking the time to read this book ahead of launch day. I sincerely appreciate your help in giving this book the launch it deserves to help such a deserving cause. You are all amazing.

Also By This Author:

This women's fiction series focuses on various aspects of mental health and overcoming trauma. It addresses anxiety, depression, panic disorders, miscarriage, adoption, grief and loss, racism, descrimination, and more, but in a light hearted way that will also make you laugh. The entire series is set in Muskoka/Bracebridge, Ontario.

Visit my website to find coordinating journal and planners.

Suburban Watchdogs: Long-time friends, Justin, Morrie, Brendon, and Josh, live in a small farming town north of the big city. When crime starts making its way onto their streets, the group of men brought together by circumstance, rather than choice, band together to keep their town safe. One movie night watching a good ol' gangster film is all they need to motivate them to take action, thereby forming the Suburban Watchdogs. If criminals think they can just waltz into the Suburban Watchdogs' territory without resistance, they are mistaken.

Justin takes matters one step further by adopting Karma. Karma is a... female dog, and she'll make sure you get what's coming to you.

Join the group of unlikely friends and their canine companion on their hilarious vigilante mission and laugh at the chaos and mayhem that ensues.

A New Leash on Life Series:
Coming Spring, 2022

This series will consist of sixteen interconnected standalone romantic comedies. Some characters from Suburban Watchdogs and the You Are Enough series will have cameos or their own starring role!

Sign up for my newsletter or follow me on social media to learn more.

Linktr.ee/burdenofproofreading

Printed in Great Britain
by Amazon

24334726R00086